PERFECTLY FLAWED
A Gentlemen of Worth Historical Romance

Shirley Marks

Finding a husband proves difficult for Lady Charlotte Worth, second daughter of the Duke of Faraday. Charlotte has every desirable attribute of a young Regency miss making her entrée into society. Eligible gentlemen cannot wait for her to make her London debut and arrive at her country house, Faraday Hall. They all speak to her of their undying love and promise a lifetime of devotion. But for Charlotte, who sees the good in everyone, this makes the decision all the more difficult.

Lady Muriel, the youngest Worth sister, is not convinced by words alone. She plans to put these gentlemen to the test, hoping there is one among them who is worthy of her sister's affection. It will take a true man of quality to look beyond Charlotte's exterior perfection and treasure her for her inner beauty.

AVALON BOOKS

PERFECTLY FLAWED

•

Shirley Marks

AVALON BOOKS
NEW YORK

Library of Congress Cataloging-in-Publication Data

Marks, Shirley.
  Perfectly flawed : a gentlemen of worth historical
romance / Shirley Marks.
      p. cm.
  ISBN 978-0-8034-7606-6 (hardcover : acid-free
paper)   1. Aristocracy (Social class)—England—
Fiction.   2. London (England)—Fiction.   I. Title.
  PS3613.A7655P47 2011
  813'.6—dc22
                                    2011018710

PRINTED IN THE UNITED STATES OF AMERICA
ON ACID-FREE PAPER
BY RR DONNELLEY, BLOOMSBURG, PENNSYLVANIA

*To my little cousin Char-Char and
my aunt Charlotte for their inspiration*

Chapter One

May 1813. Bloxwich village near Faraday Hall, Essex.

It is the height of the Season and there are no desirable, eligible gentlemen in Town. I cannot say where they have gone.

Lady Charlotte Worth recalled her aunt Mary's words from the letter she received just that morning. Charlotte leaned forward to peer out the chintz-draped window of the coach to see a throng congregating at the front door of the local assembly room.

The crowd of gentlemen, for they were all men with not a lady among them, blocked the entrance. All manner of carriages lined both sides of the main street. Charlotte had never seen so much activity in their little village before.

Could this be where the gentlemen who were supposed to be in London for the Season had migrated?

The Faraday-crested coach rolled past the front of the

assembly room and turned the corner before coming to a stop. The carriage door opened. Mr. Ogden helped the Duke of Faraday's family disembark.

Her younger sister Muriel stepped out of the coach first, followed by their aunt, Mrs. Penny Parker. Finally, Charlotte emerged and drew her cloak snugly around her. She thought it odd that they should arrive at the rear of the establishment when they had never done so before.

"Did you see how many people were out there?" Muriel remarked to no one in particular.

"That's sure enough a riot at the front portal, ladies. Best you steer clear," Mr. Ogden told them.

"I think that is the wisest course." Aunt Penny motioned for her nieces to follow her, and they stepped back from the carriage before it pulled away.

"Don't know why the gents have all flocked to our fair Bloxwich when they might roost in London." Mr. Ogden limped to the door. "It'll be standin' room only tonight, I'm afraid. Half of them will be turned away, for sure. Never saw such a crush as this in all my days!"

Charlotte noticed the worried expression creasing her aunt's brow and turned to Mr. Ogden. "Why do you suppose there are so many guests this evening?"

"They all come to meet you, Lady Charlotte." A kind smile brightened his full, round face. He held the door open for the three newly arrived guests. "Somehows they know you've been attendin' the local assembly since a few months back, and all of them want to dance with you, I s'pect."

"All of them?" Charlotte felt the blood drain from her

face. "That's quite impossible." There were not enough dances in one evening to accommodate the men lined up in the street and congregating at the front door.

"Aunt Mary did say Town was thin of men," Muriel unnecessarily reminded her sister. "I suppose we have discovered their whereabouts."

"Perhaps we should not go inside," Charlotte suggested. The crowd she'd seen gathering in front of the establishment frightened her.

"Oh, don't be so hen-hearted, Char-Char," Muriel scolded, pulling her cloak over her shoulders as if readying herself to march into battle.

"Not all of us can have the courage of the great Roman general Alexander the Great, Moo." Aunt Penny made the appeal by referring to Muriel's admiration of the Roman hero and her fascination of all things Latin.

"Alexander was Greek, not Roman. Besides, Scipio Africanus had half the army and bested him at the Battle of Zama," Muriel informed them both.

"The fact remains that each general had a dozen or more legions behind them for support. Char-Char has only the two of us." Aunt Penny would no more push Charlotte into facing her fear of the growing crowd than allow the fifteen-year-old Muriel to win this argument.

"They were at *war*," Muriel replied, nearly staring down her aunt, "not facing an adoring crowd. I cannot see how it is a reasonable comparison."

No matter how well Aunt Penny had argued on Charlotte's behalf, Charlotte herself decided they had both been correct. She could not very well have them climb back into the carriage and return to Faraday Hall simply because she did not wish to face the men who waited to dance with her.

No matter how many there were, after all, there could not be *legions* of men as Alexander had. That would be very silly indeed.

"Very well, we must go in," Charlotte said, putting on a brave front, but her insides quaked, and she hoped her fear did not show. "I thank you for accompanying me, Moo. I know how you detest attending these gatherings."

"Good for you, Char-Char." Muriel held her head high, approving of her sister's bravery. "You know I will always be near if you should need me."

"Aunt Penny? We will continue on, if you please." Charlotte pulled the fingers of her kid gloves taut, a nervous habit. She could tear the delicate stitching if she were not careful.

"If that is what you have decided, dear." Supportive Aunt Penny would see that no harm ever came to either niece.

The smile her aunt offered told Charlotte she had the right of it and they should push onward. Her aunt and her sister were her legions marching by her side.

"If you need anythin', my lady, you call ole Ogden to come, alright?"

"Thank you, Mr. Ogden." In gratitude, Charlotte matched the nod of his head with her own. She led the way through the back door of the assembly room.

Charlotte came to an abrupt stop in the main corridor upon hearing the male shouts and the violent thumps shaking the adjacent walls.

"Do you think those are sounds from an adoring crowd?" Charlotte whispered, glancing about, looking for the source of the noise. "Just listen."

The voices became louder, slashing through the air around them, turning angry. Aunt Penny winced at the scuffling noises and the sound of splintering wood. Muriel startled at a sudden shatter of porcelain, perhaps occurring in the very room next to where they stood.

"Let us continue, shall we?" Aunt Penny led the way to the cloakroom, where they removed their outer garments.

"Do not worry, Char-Char," said Muriel, straightening Charlotte's puce overskirt rather than her own green muslin. "One can always count on a good deal of chaos and unrest when too many men are about."

Charlotte arranged her sister's ringlets, allowing them to lie more attractively around her face. Attending the local assembly would benefit her sister as well. In a few years' time, Muriel will have changed her mind regarding the opposite sex, and will wish to make a favorable impression upon young men.

"Are you ready, girls?" Aunt Penny asked, continuing down the corridor. Just around the corner, they'd enter the main room where the guests gathered to dance.

Charlotte linked her arm in Muriel's and pulled her sister near as they followed their aunt. "I remember when

Gusta's suitors came for the house party. There were many gentlemen in attendance. I know it was so she could become better acquainted with each of them—as did we all, far more than we expected. They were all so tall and handsome."

"But not always well-behaved," Muriel added.

Charlotte had to agree. The house party had been two years ago and she, now eighteen, was the same age her elder sister Augusta had been. Charlotte hoped she was less naive, having learned some things when it came to being in the company of adoring suitors.

The trio reached the door and, after they were announced, the once noisy room hushed. Every eye, from every man, focused upon her.

Charlotte smiled and gazed about the room, taking in the finely dressed young men. At first glance these gentlemen appeared far better turned out than the males who'd attended the previous months' assemblies.

The print of their waistcoats and the fit of their jackets were far superior. But though the cut of their clothing was much improved, the men looked a bit creased and had an overall rumpled aspect about them.

Upon closer inspection, the gentleman in the exquisite blue superfine jacket not only had a darkened eye, he seemed to be missing two shiny buttons from his garment.

The gentleman next to him sported a large bruise on his cheek in addition to missing the left pocket from his waistcoat, which he tried to hide, unsuccessfully, by holding the front of his jacket together.

The music struck up for the interval before the first dance. Charlotte led her sister by the arm, keeping to the path behind their aunt.

Muriel, whom Charlotte considered far more observant than herself, must have also noticed the unsettling appearance of these gentlemen.

"Although they are, on the whole, handsome," Charlotte whispered to her sister, gazing at the men, "they're not very pretty, are they, Moo?"

Looking across the room and down the whole line, she further noticed swollen, lopsided lips and reddened jaws among most of the male guests. A good number of them exhibited torn jacket seams, crumpled shirt points, and cravats gone askew. The state of their attire was a crime against man! How could these men appear in public dressed this way?

"Gracious me!" she finally realized. "I do believe these men have resorted to fisticuffs."

Muriel had almost not recognized Sir Thomas Granville. It had been years since she'd seen him, but his fine aquiline nose seemed to have been recently broken. She was quite certain tomorrow he would be sporting the blackest of eyes of any gentleman present. And that was quite something, for she spotted no less than half a dozen men contending for that honor.

What were these men about? Fighting at the assembly room? Make no mistake, she had heard them, and so had her aunt and her sister. Charlotte had commented as much upon their entrance.

Muriel noticed a man with wavy blond hair, one of the few faces without a blemish, approaching Charlotte.

"Please, Lady Charlotte," he uttered with a sigh and bowed. "I beg you remember me, Lord Carlton Wingate. Do you recall our meeting nearly two years ago?" He did not pause long enough for her to reply. "I remember as if it were yesterday. You were merely a young lady of sixteen. Now, at eighteen, you are even more lovely to behold."

If Muriel was not mistaken, his eyes were filling with tears.

"I cannot imagine how it is possible that you have grown more beautiful since last we met." He gazed upon her face, her hair, and her dress with admiration.

"I recall watching him being escorted *from* the Music Room at Faraday Hall during Augusta's house party," Aunt Penny told Muriel in a soft voice, the comment meant for her ears alone. "He became quite emotional over Charlotte's harp playing."

"I have been waiting for this day for a very, very long time," he continued, clearing his throat and blinking aside the emotion that threatened to overtake his voice. Lord Carlton made a cursory glance around and then straightened. "I see there is no one brave enough, or perhaps worthy enough, to step out with you. May *I* have the privilege of asking for your first dance?"

Muriel realized that her sister could not very well turn him down if she wished to dance at all tonight. Surprising as it seemed, Charlotte accepted, appearing entirely delighted for the opportunity.

Lord Carlton had never looked happier as he led Charlotte to the dance floor.

Muriel regarded Charlotte's flawless visage. In the sunlight her radiant blond hair appeared guinea gold. In the flattering candlelight of the assembly room, it might have appeared she wore a shimmering halo about her head. How could any man resist such beauty?

Charlotte with Lord Carlton, both flaxen-haired, made quite the golden couple. The sight of them seemed to spur the other gentlemen into action. They wasted no additional time in approaching Aunt Penny, asking for an introduction and a dance with the fair Charlotte.

By evening's end, there would be many unhappy men and one exhausted sister who conversed with more gentlemen than she could count on both hands and who took part in every dance. Unfortunately, there would never be enough dances for every young man who wished to partner Charlotte this night.

At promptly ten o'clock the next morning, Muriel followed Aunt Penny down the main staircase to the Grand Foyer. Her aunt paused, watching the butler pull the front door open wide, which revealed a very presentable Lord Carlton Wingate.

"Is Lady Charlotte at home?" Lord Carlton handed his calling card to Huxley.

The butler accepted the card and admitted the visitor. "I shall inquire, my lord."

Aunt Penny motioned for Muriel to stay while she continued forward. "It is not as if I am not pleased to see you," she said. "I am merely surprised because I wasn't expecting anyone quite this early."

It was quite early for a morning call. Aunt Penny must have excused his impertinence because they were in the country and not keeping Town hours.

"I do beg your pardon." He bowed. Despite the hour, Lord Carlton had not neglected his appearance. Immaculately dressed in a dark blue jacket, gold-striped waistcoat, and buff trousers, his blond hair gleamed, giving him the appearance of a very serious suitor who had taken great pains in dressing for his visit. "If I had not arrived now, I may not have been fortunate enough to have the audience with Lady Charlotte that I desire."

"I am sure there is no need to rush," Aunt Penny said, sounding nearly as nervous as Lord Carlton appeared. Muriel could see his hands gripping and crushing the brim of his hat, in nervousness, she supposed.

"I had hoped that—" He stopped and blinked, looking uncertain. "Well, that is to say—" He broke off again and cleared his throat. "I wish to express my affection and make my intentions known to Lady Charlotte."

"Do you not think it a bit soon for that, sir?" Aunt Penny snapped at him. His declaration shocked Muriel as well.

"I would like to discuss an offer of marriage." Lord Carlton stood very tall with newfound confidence, making it evident he would not be dissuaded.

"You cannot!" Aunt Penny told him. "It is impossible to accept your offer, in any case, since the Duke is not present. I suggest you delay your proposal until such time as you can speak to His Grace."

"Wait? I have been waiting for these past two years . . . I have been most patient and faithful. I beg that I have a chance to win her heart!" Lord Carlton's voice rose, although it held a slight emotional quaver.

"There is nothing for it, sir. You *will* have to wait. You have no choice." Aunt Penny stood up to him, not allowing him to bully her. "The offer for marriage must be put forth to the Duke. If you wish to see Lady Charlotte, you must remain belowstairs until she awakens."

"Very well." He strode to the wall of Sheraton chairs on one side of the Grand Foyer and lowered himself onto the seat with great dignity and an air of stubbornness. "I shall remain fixed here until Lady Charlotte arrives."

Chapter Two

Charlotte sat in bed having her morning chocolate. She had had such a splendid time last night, dancing every dance and talking with so many gentlemen, that she could not remember who was whom after the long evening. Even after a full night's sleep, she felt fatigued. She still had a few days to rest before leaving for London at the end of the week.

There was a light rap on her bedchamber door before it was pushed open. Muriel leaned in and called to her, "Char-Char?"

"Moo?" Charlotte leaned forward. "Come in, please. Oh, and Aunt Penny . . . Is there something wrong?" For both to arrive before she had risen must be an indication of some trouble indeed.

"Dear, I do not mean to cause you distress," her aunt told her. "But Lord Carlton is belowstairs and insists upon seeing you."

"Lord Carlton Wingate?" Charlotte handed her cup of chocolate to her aunt and readied herself to rise from the bed. Charlotte felt terrible. Here she lay idle, wasting Lord Carlton's time, making him wait for her. "Why has he called so early?"

Muriel stood at the window, gazing outside, and remained silent.

"Lord Carlton may not be your only visitor today, Char-Char," said Aunt Penny, as she set the Dresden china cup aside to help her niece out of bed. "There were so many gentlemen and not nearly enough sets to accommodate them. Since they could not all dance with you last night, I told them they should feel free to call during the next few days."

"Exactly how many did you say this to?" inquired Charlotte.

Muriel spoke over her shoulder to her relatives, transfixed on the view before her. "There are a good two dozen or so gentlemen on their way here now, I'd say."

"What?" Aunt Penny left Charlotte's bedside, moving to the window.

"There's a long line of carriages, and many more men on horseback, coming down the road in our direction." Muriel need not have described the unusual sight, as Aunt Penny was standing next to her in a thrice. Charlotte flung her covers aside and leaped out of bed to see for herself.

"Oh, no!" Aunt Penny stared at the gentlemen who would soon be descending upon Faraday Hall.

"Look how many there are," said Charlotte, staring out the window. Far off in the distance she could see the line of carriages.

The three remained quiet for several moments.

"We were to leave for Town by week's end," Aunt Penny finally said. "But if all the eligible gentlemen are here—it is just as your aunt Mary had written to us."

"And we can see as much for ourselves," Muriel added.

"There is no need to travel to town, is there?" Aunt Penny said, sounding as if she were faced with a conundrum.

Charlotte could not believe her dream of going to London for the theater and parties, and visiting the infamous assembly rooms of Almack's, would be for naught. It appeared she was to remain in the country instead of partaking in the gaiety of the Season.

"If the eligibles are here, I wonder what types of males remain behind." Muriel mused aloud.

"Not anyone with whom we would care to rub elbows—young bloods, ne'er-do-wells, and wastrels who frequent clubs and have more interest in gambling than courting young ladies." Aunt Penny swept Charlotte's unbound hair behind her shoulders, indicating she had indeed referred to her niece.

"It is a shame they cannot stay here, as Augusta had her suitors attend our house party after the Season," said Charlotte, but she knew this was a suggestion that could not be realized.

"Only gentlemen?" Aunt Penny seemed to consider the notion, but it was obvious she did not like it. "Oh, no. We cannot have only gentlemen as guests. That would not be proper at all. They simply must remain where they are. There is nothing for it."

Aunt Penny sounded a bit worried, and more than a bit apprehensive. "I think I had best write your father. I realize he is occupied, with Parliament in session, but he might think it more important to return home to deal with family matters."

"What about having the gentlemen to supper?" Charlotte suggested, hoping for a more acceptable solution to their problem at hand.

"We still need to invite some women," Aunt Penny replied. "All the young ladies who are *out* are in Town. There are no eligible ladies remaining to invite for supper or for a ball, for that matter. This is all quite vexing."

"What if we had the gentlemen for tea?" Charlotte put forth.

"We certainly could manage that, don't you think? We could have Cook make some small cakes, tarts, biscuits, and assorted savories." Aunt Penny seemed agreeable to the notion. "That certainly sounds manageable."

"Especially if we reduce their number down to a half dozen or so," said Muriel. "I'm not yet sure how we are to accomplish such a feat." It appeared Muriel, whom Charlotte considered so very clever, was coming up with one of her ideas. "I own there must be a way. It would be better yet if it could be done where we need not do the pruning."

"Only six?" Aunt Penny sounded somewhat taken aback. "How can we possibly manage that?"

"I am not yet entirely sure. I shall first see to the simpler task of removing just one," she said, stepping away from the two and making her departure. "You may stand here and watch from the window, if that is what you like."

Charlotte did not exactly know what her sister would do but dreaded what would happen next. "We must stop her!" She made to dash out the door in pursuit, but Aunt Penny took hold of her arm.

"I think it best we allow Muriel to continue." Aunt Penny led Charlotte to the window for a view of the parterre below.

There must be a better, kinder way to discourage a man. Charlotte then remembered poor Lord Carlton who waited in the Grand Foyer.

"Oh, no. I'm sure Moo is going to be absolutely wretched to Lord Carlton and cause him to flee!"

Muriel descended the staircase to find Lord Carlton Wingate perched upon one of the many chairs in the Grand Foyer, waiting for Charlotte to appear.

He rose upon her arrival and bowed. "Good day to you, Lady Muriel."

"May I have a word with you, my lord?"

"Of course." He glanced about for Charlotte. Muriel decided she would keep it to herself that her sister would not be joining them.

"If you would please follow me." Muriel intended to lead him out of the house for, hopefully, the final time.

"I dare not leave," he insisted, refusing to step a foot away from his chair. "I await Lady Charlotte."

"That is exactly what I wish to speak to you about,

my lord," Muriel confided to him. "She will not make an appearance for at least an hour."

A lackluster "Oh" was his reply. Clearly he did not like the news of another hour's wait. "Very well, then."

Muriel led the way down the corridor and out the side door to the parterre, where her sister and her aunt could watch the proceedings from Charlotte's bedchamber.

"I would like to come straight to the point if I might, my lord," Muriel began. "This may sound forward, but I need to know if you truly believe you have a chance to win my sister's affection."

"A chance?" He seemed surprised by her question. "Excuse me for sounding perhaps a bit confident regarding my station, but my father is the Marquess of Albany." He stood straighter and held his head higher with pride at the announcement.

"Yes, that's what I understand—a noble family," she agreed, and allowed a note of doubt to trickle into her voice. Lord Carlton had come from a fine family; there was no doubt about that.

"Yes, one of the noblest," he stated with pride.

"And you are a younger son—one of four, if I recall— and the youngest. So there is really no chance of coming into your father's title, is there?" Muriel wrinkled her nose and smoothed her hair with two fingers. "Quite a shame, really."

Lord Carlton mumbled something. Muriel pretended not to hear his protest.

"Well, I must say there are all types of men Charlotte

has to choose from. There are the rich"—she ticked off on her finger—"and then there are those who are *extremely* rich. Some of the gentlemen are handsome and some are *prodigiously* handsome, indeed." Muriel sighed, displaying a smile proving that she, too, had been captivated by the very same gentlemen. "Most of them are titled or will come into their family titles. There are not many younger sons, mind you, but they are all younger men."

Lord Carlton's hand-wringing did not go unnoticed. If Muriel was not mistaken, it seemed his face had grown a bit redder with mounting frustration regarding her observations of his competitors.

"I am not . . . no, indeed, I am not all *that* old." His uncertainty and the strain he felt was evident, lacing through his tone. It sounded as if he did not even believe his own words.

"Of course not," Muriel cooed with a smile, doing her best to imitate Charlotte's agreeable manner, the one that seemed to please gentlemen. "If I am not mistaken, you were six and twenty when you courted my sister Augusta."

She looked at him for confirmation. He did not give it, but by his obvious omission, Muriel assumed she must have been right.

"That would make you now . . . *eight* and twenty? Oh, dear, *nearly* thirty years of age. Really? Oh, that cannot be correct." Muriel glanced at him as if she simply could not believe she had calculated the sum properly. "Charlotte, who is eighteen years of age, will not mind a difference of a mere ten years," she said to reassure him, but not in a wholly confident tone.

"There are many marriages whose husbands and wives share such a discrepancy in age—*more* of an age difference, in fact," Lord Carlton stated with certainty. But something about him, the slight slouch of his shoulders, the crease between his brows, or the downturn of his mouth, conveyed that he felt more than a bit uneasy.

"Of course, you are correct," she quickly agreed, thinking of arranged marriages where the bride did not have a choice in whom they married. "I am sure that if Charlotte were *truly* in love with a gentleman, even if he were more than a decade older . . . it would not matter to her in the least."

Muriel paused and narrowed her eyes to give the impression she was considering the matter—believed it, even. Her reaction did not seem to lend Lord Carlton comfort.

"As a young lady approaching a marriageable age myself," she muttered, as if allowing him to hear her innermost thoughts, "I believe it might be easier, on the whole, to fall in love with a younger man."

"But I am here *now,* young lady." The uncharacteristic sternness in his voice did not frighten Muriel. "And I wish to pay my addresses."

Muriel tilted her head and batted her lashes, as she had seen Charlotte do many times. "I do not think you dare suggest marriage to her, not without speaking to our father first. No, I cannot see it done."

Lord Carlton was beginning to quake, but still no

crack in his already shaken self-confidence was in sight. She needed to continue a bit longer.

"It is true that you are the first to arrive and, perhaps, the first who wishes to make an offer but, sadly, I do not believe you are alone."

"What?" came his choked response. "I beg your pardon. I do not believe I—"

"There." Muriel pointed off into the distance, to his left. "Do you see? Charlotte's young men are coming to call."

Lord Carlton's eyes widened upon seeing the long line of carriages and men on horseback approaching Faraday Hall. An expression of horror washed across his blanching face.

"Oh, no." He clasped his hands together, pleading with her. "Please, you must allow me to see her, to speak to her. I must tell her—"

"I'm afraid that will not be possible." A twinge of guilt passed through Muriel. She really disliked having to resort to something so . . . sinister, but this would be the best for Lord Carlton, really.

"I shan't have a chance with her . . . not with those *others* paying her court." Lord Carlton Wingate dropped onto his knees before Muriel. It was not a romantic gesture but one that spoke of pure desperation. "I cannot see how I am to have a chance with her unless I am the first to tell her of my devotion and how much I adore her. I must convince her to become my wife before the others arrive."

From her bedchamber, Charlotte looked at the scene

playing out below. "I do hope Moo is not being too harsh with him."

"I really should have been the one speaking to Lord Carlton," Aunt Penny confessed, not sounding particularly proud of herself.

"If Moo were here and you were there, she could tell me exactly what is transpiring," Charlotte noted.

"I am not always pleased when she eavesdrops," said Aunt Penny, keeping a firm hold on Charlotte's arm, "but there are times when her talent is quite valuable."

"But then, one need not know his exact words. It is quite apparent that he is in great distress." Charlotte could not help but empathize with him.

Lord Carlton knelt before Muriel, his fingers intertwined in a tight grip.

"Poor Lord Carlton." Charlotte's words were heartfelt. "He is not enjoying their tête-à-tête."

"But I can understand your sister's point in discouraging him." Aunt Penny must have felt sorry for him as well.

Muriel drew out linen from her sleeve and offered it to Lord Carlton. His chin dropped onto his chest, and it was quite clear that again he had broken down into tears, which seemed to be a common occurrence.

Aunt Penny remarked, "Honestly, the man really must learn to carry his own handkerchief."

Chapter Three

Out of the corner of her eye, Charlotte spied Muriel and Aunt Penny standing at her window not long after Lord Carlton's departure. They seemed obsessed with the long line of travelers nearing the estate grounds.

"They came all this way to see me." Charlotte remarked, sitting at the dressing table while their abigail, Lydia, fussed over her toilette.

Charlotte had planned to wear a blue spencer over her lovely Vandyke-lace–embellished, petal-colored morning gown. Lydia insisted she make a special effort with her hair since more than a dozen callers would soon arrive.

All of them wished to catch her eye. How was that possible? The thought of so many gentlemen calling on her was nearly overwhelming; that she should disappoint any one of them caused her to fret. She must do something to ensure each one had an equal chance to have a word with her, to exchange glances or a smile.

"The least I can do is make time for them," Charlotte announced, coming to a decision.

"Well, of course you will, dear," Aunt Penny replied with no notion what Charlotte had in mind.

"I do wonder how the other gentlemen will tolerate such an arrangement," said Charlotte, sitting perfectly still, allowing Lydia to complete the final touches with the hot iron.

"What are you talking about, Char-Char?" Muriel stepped away from the window and stared at her sister.

"I wish to give each of the gentlemen who calls ten or so minutes of my undivided attention." Charlotte was completely serious. "Allow them some time when they do not need to compete with one another for my attention. It is the least I can do for them."

"It will require a good portion of your day if you were to allow each time of their own." Muriel must have quickly tallied the sum. "That will take hours!"

"I am well aware of that, Moo." Charlotte, who would not move from her decision, stared into the mirror at the reflection of her sister, standing behind her. "Do you not see that these gentlemen have given up their Season to come here? And I cannot possibly encourage all of them." Lydia stood by with the straw bonnet in her hand while Charlotte pulled on her pale lemon-colored kid gloves and announced, "It is something I must do."

The gentlemen reached Faraday Hall at approximately two o'clock in the afternoon. Huxley admitted them one after the other. Soon the Grand Foyer was brimming with suitors for Charlotte.

"This is ridiculous," Muriel complained to Aunt Penny,

who had led Charlotte belowstairs to welcome her suitors, and then retreated up one floor to observe the entire mass. They stood at the railing on the first floor, looking down. "The whole lot of them will be smelling of April and May, including Char-Char."

"An entire houseful of men in love with Charlotte?" mused Aunt Penny, appearing light-headed at the thought. "I'm not sure exactly what we can do about it. We certainly cannot choose a husband for her."

"I suppose we must make the best of this situation." Muriel could not bear the thought of her sister choosing the wrong man.

"There are simply too many men," Aunt Penny said bluntly. "If we do not gain some semblance of order, there will soon be bedlam."

"Perhaps Char-Char's idea is a sound one, after all." Muriel knew she was not the only member of the family who could come up with resolutions to their problems.

Aunt Penny descended the stairs, stopping three steps from the ground floor, which put her a good head taller than the tallest man in attendance.

"Excuse me, gentlemen! Gentlemen, if I may have your attention." Aunt Penny waited until the crowd quieted before continuing. She held up a sheet of paper. "If you all will be so good as to add your name in the order in which you arrived, Lady Charlotte would like to stroll with you through the back gardens. Yes, that's right, sirs, each and every one of you, if you will all be so kind to wait your turn."

The gentlemen stepped toward her aunt, following

her instructions, lining up to add their names to the list. Muriel noticed Charlotte's attention was sidetracked by local baronet Sir Nicholas Petersham, who took the opportunity to make introductions for two young men who had accompanied him.

"Lady Charlotte, may I present to you Lord Irving and Sir Hugh Linville?"

"How do you do? If you two gentlemen wish to add your names to the list my aunt presently amasses"— Charlotte indicated behind her, off to her left—"over by the round table, I would gladly take a turn through our lovely family gardens with each of you as well."

"Yes, of course," Lord Irving agreed at the same time that Sir Hugh replied, "I shall gladly do so at once."

Charlotte graciously made her exit to collect her straw bonnet and confer with Aunt Penny.

"Did I or did I not say that Lady Charlotte was the loveliest creature upon this earth?" Sir Nicholas intoned. Clearly he had been talking up Charlotte's virtues to these two gentlemen.

Muriel waited for Sir Nicholas' payoff. It seemed to her he never approached matters in a straightforward manner. For him there always seemed to be some wager involved.

"Yes, absolutely. Rightly so," declared Sir Hugh. Lord Irving stood there, remaining as silent as he had upon making Charlotte's acquaintance.

"Pay up, gents." Sir Nicholas held out his palm, into which they each slipped a coin.

Muriel huffed with indignation. Sir Nicholas Petersham was one of the most unscrupulous cads she could ever imagine. Then the notion came to her that he might prove useful.

Three and three-quarters of an hour later, Charlotte swept into the Citrus Parlor fatigued from her numerous turns about the grounds.

"Sukey, see our Char-Char has arrived," Muriel called out, rising from her chair.

"Char-Char, have you finished, finally?" Miss Susan Wilbanks leaped up to collect Charlotte's straw bonnet and lead the latecomer to her seat. Susan, the younger sister of Richard and Emily, grew up on the neighboring property, Yewhill Grange.

"Oh, do sit," said Muriel, quick to pour Charlotte a cup of tea. "Perhaps what you truly need is a bucket of warm water to soak your feet."

Charlotte eased into her chair and relaxed.

"Do not tell me you accompanied each and every one of those gentlemen through the rear gardens." Susan settled onto her seat next to Charlotte.

"Very well, I shan't say it if you do not wish to hear." Charlotte accepted the teacup from Muriel with a pleasant smile. "Thank you so much, Moo. I am certain this will make me feel just the thing."

"Is it true you are not going to Town? Not at all?" It seemed Susan could not make sense of what had happened that afternoon, nor of what changes were to be made because of it. "That is where your cousin Miriam found a husband, and he's an earl!"

"That is beside the point. There is no need for Char-

Char to travel to London when *all* the men are here," Muriel told Susan, who was much closer to her age than Charlotte's.

"If Papa and Aunt Penny think it best I remain in the country, then I shall." Charlotte sighed and glanced from the rim of her cup to the plate of small cakes sitting on the table just to the right of Muriel.

"Allow me," said Muriel, retrieving the dish and offering Charlotte a cake. "I believe Papa is on his way home to manage the influx of gentlemen who have descended upon us."

"Yes, there are so many." Apparently Susan continued to have difficulty with the concept of London gentlemen inhabiting their small village of Bloxwich. "His Grace, yes, he could set things to right."

Charlotte placed her teacup upon its saucer ever so lightly, so as not to risk injuring the fine Dresden china, and then selected one of the cakes. "Thank you, Moo. I honestly cannot believe I am this famished."

"I expect you really need not travel to Town. The country is also where both our beloved Gusta and Em found their husbands," Susan declared. "I suppose it must be possible for you to do so as well."

Aunt Penny entered, appearing as fatigued as Charlotte, and joined the gathering. Muriel moved to fetch her a cup of tea.

"Not right now, dear," said Aunt Penny, staying Muriel's effort with the wave of her hand. "I need a few moments to just sit. What an afternoon it has been!"

"I am sorry to have put you through that ordeal, Aunt

Penny." Guilt swept through Charlotte. Not only had she endured the long afternoon, but Aunt Penny had as well, remaining until the last gentleman departed.

"Do not feel as if you have caused me any pains at all, my dearest Char-Char. I had no knowledge of it then, but now that the day has played out, I believe your solution was most sensible. There was not one disagreement among all your gentlemen callers. Not one fist or voice was raised all afternoon. All of them behaved like . . . gentlemen. I am quite amazed and pleased at their behavior."

"I, too, am pleased." Charlotte gazed into her teacup and a smile came to her lips. The gentlemen were delightful company. "I abhor quarreling above all and I will not abide their fighting."

"Do not say they were actually striking one another?" Susan looked from Muriel to Charlotte.

Charlotte nodded.

"You cannot like that," Susan agreed. "Tell me, Char-Char, is there not one or two that you favor among them?"

"No, I do not believe I do." Charlotte tilted her head and seemingly gazed toward the window to find her answer. "How can I possibly? They each have unique admirable qualities to recommend them and each one is a fine gentleman indeed."

"You see, *that* is the difficulty." Muriel needed to point out the obvious because, until someone came up with a solution for the dilemma, they would continue to have too many men at Faraday Hall.

"How shall we occupy them tomorrow?" asked Aunt

Penny, appearing to welcome anyone to voice an answer. They needed a solution.

"Tomorrow? You don't expect them all to return, do you?" Muriel looked from her aunt to her sister.

Both Charlotte and Aunt Penny shrugged and neither commented.

"We cannot allow pandemonium," Muriel stated emphatically. "That is what could have happened today."

Those were exactly Charlotte's thoughts.

"I think it best if we limit the number of suitors," Muriel suggested.

"I won't have to choose, will I?" Charlotte's eyes widened and grew moist. She hated to think of the others she would disappoint. "I do not think I can possibly manage that. How can I possibly choose among them? It would be most unfair."

"I wasn't thinking you should need to," said Muriel. By the look on her face, she had a plan in the works.

"Why would it matter?" said Susan. "Choose a half dozen or so—Char-Char likes them all."

"Yes, we can invite six for tea," Muriel continued. "Instead of us choosing, each of the gentlemen will have to *earn* their spot."

"Earn? How?" Charlotte straightened, interested in her sister's plan. "I must admit it would be a great help if there were a way to limit the number of callers."

"If we could have them perform a task that would make a few of them stand out . . ." Muriel fell quiet for a few moments and then burst out with excitement, nearly frightening them. "Fruit tarts, biscuits, and scones!"

"You don't propose we have the gentlemen bake for us?" Charlotte uttered in surprise. "We might all regret feasting where the gentlemen, as agreeable and handsome as they are, have had a hand in the food preparation."

"No, no. I do not mean we should go quite that far." Muriel stifled her laughter. "We'll have the gentlemen pick berries for us, for Charlotte. Her favorite ones."

"It's a bit early for gooseberries, don't you think?" Aunt Penny sat back in her chair.

"Not in the patch on Owl Hill to the south," said Muriel. It seemed she had thought her plan out. "We always find the first ripe berries of the season there. Even now some will be ready, perhaps not many; I'm sure there will be enough. The first six gentlemen who fill their pails will be invited to take tea with Charlotte."

Charlotte liked the idea immediately. How clever her sister was to have thought of giving the men a quest.

Aunt Penny, however, gave her youngest niece's suggestion more thought before asking, "And how, exactly, would we notify the gentlemen of this task?"

Muriel smiled. "I thought I would enlist the help of a man whose very life's passion is to create a gaming environment—Sir Nicholas Petersham."

"Moo"—Aunt Penny smiled and exhaled, sounding as if she were completely at ease now—"I believe I am ready for that cup of tea."

Chapter Four

Muriel had been quite correct. If there were even a hint of profitable sport, Sir Nicholas Petersham would most heartedly wish to be included. His talents would be put to good use. He said he was delighted to be of service to the Duke of Faraday, when Aunt Penny, on behalf of the family, contacted him.

Sir Nicholas answered the summons several hours later. Aunt Penny, Muriel, and Charlotte were there to greet him. Muriel laid out her plan before them all.

She would bring the small pails, provided by the kitchen, which the gentlemen would fill with ripe gooseberries. They would be baked and then served at tea for Charlotte and the first six gentlemen, along with Aunt Penny, Muriel, Susan Wilbanks, and Sir Nicholas.

Sir Nicholas agreed to pass on the contest details to the gentlemen in the village. The following day, he would lead the interested parties to the arranged meeting place.

The next morning at ten, Muriel met the local baronet and the nearly two dozen men he brought with him to The Wild Rose Inn. Muriel dressed in a sedate sprigged muslin and a straw chip to shield her face from the sun. Crawford, one of the kitchen staff, accompanied her, along with a goodly number of tin pails. They led the way to the top of the hill, driving along in her pony cart pulled by Buttercup.

Sir Nicholas agreed to serve as referee to assure the gents behaved themselves and the competition was done on the up-and-up. Crawford had the final say and would assure each pail contained the proper volume of ripe berries.

Muriel left the men, who were anxious to begin their gooseberry hunt, in the care of Sir Nicholas.

Satisfied that the task would continue as planned, Muriel boarded the pony cart and started back for Faraday Hall.

Sir Philip Somerville replaced his hat firmly on his head without regard to whether it sat at a rakish angle. He walked along the side of the dirt road, swinging his walking stick in sync with his stride and considered how, once again, his curiosity had gotten the better of him.

A scant hour ago he traveled from the north on his way to London in his curricle, of moderate age, with his excellent, newly purchased pair of matched bays. Not long after, he spied a line of travelers moving south. The large party so intrigued Philip, he gave in to temptation, altering his direction to follow them and discover their final destination.

No sooner had he turned east, not yet on the same road as the procession, when the wheel of his curricle dropped into a hole and the vehicle came to an immediate stop.

The horses lurched, nearly breaking free. Philip kept them steady with calming words and gentle hands. He descended the crippled vehicle to see to the well-being of his bays and further examine his rig. Not only had his wheel broken, but the axle had snapped. It was then he realized his journey had come to an end, but he did not doubt a new adventure was about to unfold.

"You look as if you could use some help." A trustworthy-looking fellow approached while Philip mulled over how to unhitch his team. "If I may be of service to ya, sir."

Philip straightened to reply, "I would very much appreciate the assistance. Whom do I have the honor of thanking?"

The man pulled his cap from his head and introduced himself. "Donny Ellis, sir."

The local villager took it upon himself to carry Philip's leather chest and lead the horses, with the traces hanging over his shoulder, while leaving Philip empty-handed with the exception of his walking stick.

A good twenty minutes after they had taken to foot on their way to the local village of Bloxwich, a small cart, pulled by a small pony and driven by a young lass, came rolling up behind them.

"You there," Philip called out to the girl. "Stop. Halt, I say!"

The cart slowed to a standstill and the girl regarded the sight confronting her at the side of the road.

"Good thing you come along—" Mr. Ellis began, shifting the trunk in his arms.

"Yes, yes, my good man." With his raised, York tan–gloved hand, Philip motioned to Ellis to remain quiet. There was no need to make any further arrangement. The baronet could manage from here. "We're very appreciative that the . . . young lady . . . and her . . . her transport has chance to pass." He eyed the pony and the cart, feeling thankful that she had happened by and hoping the diminutive steed would prove sufficient.

"If you'll be headed toward Faraday Hall, His Grace is a good man. He'll offer a gent such as yourself a place to stay." Ellis gestured, the best he could, toward his companion.

Philip raised his silver-topped cane. "Young miss, if you would be so good as to convey me to Faraday Hall, I would be most grateful." He motioned for Ellis to set the leather chest upon the back of the pony cart while Philip settled onto the front seat next to the driver.

The young lady obviously needed some instruction, and Philip provided it. "Onward, if you please." He indicated the forward direction with his walking stick.

She remained still and replied, "No 'thank you'?"

"We have not arrived at our destination, my dear," he teased her. "You might have failed to notice that we have yet to depart!"

"Not to *me*," she snapped. "A thank-you to Mr. Ellis, for carrying your trunk and caring for your horses."

"Yes, the fine fellow was good enough to give me a hand with my luggage and my cattle. You need not concern yourself over an appropriate expression of gratitude on my part."

Philip had no idea what age this slip of a girl was. Regardless of her plain garment and simple straw hat, she was no country lass, and he found her decorum remarkable for someone so young. What was this young lady of quality doing roaming around the countryside alone?

The gentlemanly part of him felt the need to extend his protection, see to her well-being, and the other part could not resist roasting her! It amused him to play the part of someone a bit more pretentious, if only to tease her.

Philip leaned toward her to whisper something he suspected would displease her: "He was friendly enough, but I honestly could not understand half of what he said."

The narrowing of her eyes displayed her annoyance. "I'm afraid that Mr. Ellis has been correct in assuming you might find temporary shelter at Faraday Hall. Especially since it appears your vehicle might have broken down on or near the Duke's property. It is unclear whose misfortune this truly is."

For the next thirty-five minutes she remained quiet while Philip subjected her to a full narration of the landscape and commentary of their journey, along with his opinion on both topics. Not once had she interrupted him to add her own remarks or introduce herself.

The pony cart turned a corner, approaching a man working his field up ahead. The farmer ceased his toil to wave at the passersby.

"Pull up at once, missy," the baronet ordered. The young lady reined in the pony, bringing the cart to a stop. Philip addressed the man in the field, "Excuse me, sir, might I make an inquiry?"

"Me, sir?" The man standing in the field indicated himself.

"Yes, you, sir." Philip lifted his walking stick. Sunlight gleamed off its silver lion-headed top. "Can you tell me about all this coming and going on round here? There's an abnormal number of fine rigs lining the road beyond. Tell me, sir, what goes on there?"

"Ah—don't know rightly if them the same morts as what's gone to Faraday 'All the day afore.'" The farmer wiped his forehead with a swipe of his sleeve. "Can't say where them be off to this fine mornin'."

"Faraday Hall, did you say?" It was convenient that Philip was now bound in that direction. No doubt, once there, he would be in a position to fully sate his curiosity.

"That's His Grace's, the Duke's place, it is. He's got three lover-ly girls, he does."

"Does he, now?" Philip remarked.

"That's right, he does."

With his head tilted, Philip eyed the young lady seated

next to him. Was it possible his driver was one of His Grace's offspring? "How fortunate for the Duke that he is blessed with *three* beautiful daughters."

"Right enough, that what I said!" the farmer returned.

"Not precisely, but my translation appears adequate," Philip whispered to the young lady.

"This man"—she indicated Philip with the nod of her head—"is far too polite to ask that you tell him the particulars, but he does wish to know. Mr. Gilbert, pray do go on."

What an impertinent female she is!

"The first girl's already gone, married a few years back," Farmer Gilbert said. "That was a right mess, all those fancy morts showin' up an' gettin' puffed off one by one."

"Really? How interesting," said Philip, but he could not prevent a small sigh from escaping. Apparently this young woman was capable of retaliation, bringing about as much irritation as he had caused her.

"Is Grace's middle girl . . . There's a lady, an angel, everyone thinks so. She's slipped her halo into her reticule and hidin' a pair of wings 'neath her cloak, that one does."

"Does she really?" Philip managed a polite smile, pained at having to endure the unnecessary conversation that consumed precious time. They really should have been on their way.

"A finer lady you'll never meet, m'lord. Never, I says, if you ask me."

It seemed to Philip his traveling companion thoroughly enjoyed watching him in his discomfort. He could not allow this young miss to get the best of him, so he begged another answer from the farmer, proving Philip could participate in a full and thorough conversation.

"You mentioned the Duke having three daughters? What can you tell me about the youngest? A paragon in her own right, no doubt? Surpassing her sisters, perhaps?"

The broad-faced Farmer Gilbert glanced at the girl next to Philip in the pony cart, and guffawed with a wide grin, pointing his large, dirty finger at them. "Wot there's Lady Muriel right next to you, m'lord."

Philip had suspected the very thing to be true, but even when he heard the words, he could not believe it. She was a duke's daughter. Of course she had impeccable manners. The baronet turned his head and lifted the quizzing glass dangling at the end of a ribbon he wore around his neck to regard her.

She remained quiet and tilted her chin upward to give him a splendid view of her profile.

"Lady Muriel, is it?" Keeping his face impassive, he took an extraordinary amount of time to examine his driver. Then he lied, "And I thought you a simple country bumpkin."

Muriel rolled into the stable yards at Faraday Hall with Sir Philip by her side. After the discovery of her identity, the baronet, in line to inherit the title of Earl of

Danbury upon the death of his father—who presently enjoyed exceptionally good health—deemed it necessary that he should introduce himself, despite Muriel's objection.

She would rather not know any more about him.

Aunt Penny and Charlotte met Muriel and their unexpected visitor on the terrace at the rear of the house.

"Sir Philip, this is my aunt, Mrs. Parker." Muriel turned to Aunt Penny. "Sir Ph—"

"Sir Philip Somerville, Exquisite." With a full extension and outward sweep of his arms, in what Muriel thought was a windmill-like motion, Sir Philip lifted his left knee waist high and traced a pattern with the pointed toe of his boot. He drew in a breath before lightly placing his foot before him, preparing to complete his bow.

Finishing the motion, he swept the edge of his coat with his left hand and flared the tail of his garment out to one side before artfully casting his arm forward before him.

Aunt Penny took a step back.

With a stylish flip of his right wrist, Sir Philip positioned his right arm in an arc over his head, and descended low into the bow, nearly reaching his foot.

"Goodness!" Aunt Penny cried at his lavish display, appearing to have been left a bit breathless.

"Ah, me . . ." Charlotte's eyes fluttered and she placed her hand lightly upon her throat, drawing in a labored breath.

It was probably too much flourish for a person to take in all at once. At least, it had been for Muriel. "Honestly," she whispered, unable to keep silent.

"I would not dare impose upon His Grace, Mrs. Parker, but my curricle hit a nasty hole on the road. Several spokes split and the wheel dislodged itself, sending the axle to the ground where it summarily snapped in two."

"How unfortunate," Aunt Penny commented.

"For us," Muriel added softly.

"A kind villager happened to pass by and came to my aid. Mr. Ellis will see to the care of my horses and make preliminary arrangements for my vehicle's repair on my behalf. I must attend to the final arrangements with the local wheelwright as soon as possible. I would normally obtain temporary residence in a nearby establishment, but as I understand, there is not an empty room to be had within ten miles."

"Ten miles?" Charlotte echoed, knowing the exact reason why the nearby establishments were filled.

Muriel swung her gaze from Sir Philip to her breathless sister.

"He made the suggestion," Sir Philip continued, "that because of my position and situation, I might impose upon His Grace's hospitality. It was fortunate that Lady Muriel, here, came along—most fortuitous on my part." He made a modest bow to her. "And she was in the position to relay me and my necessities forthwith."

A few moments passed in silence.

Aunt Penny blinked. "His Grace is not presently at home, but I am more than willing to extend an invitation to you on his behalf until your transportation can be repaired. We could also have the repairs done by our own—"

"I thank you"—Sir Philip held up his gloved hand—"but that will not be necessary. I'd much rather employ those whose livelihood depends on their daily toil. Honest work for honest pay, you know." He glanced at her from the corner of his eye and smiled. "I shall gladly accept your hospitality. I suppose I have no other choice but to foist my presence upon you poor, unsuspecting souls."

Muriel mumbled to herself.

"Huxley," Aunt Penny called to the butler, which may have been an effort to cover Muriel's protest. "Will you see that Sir Philip is settled in the Gold Suite?"

"I shall, madam," the butler acknowledged.

"We'll send for your luggage and your man."

"I am quite alone, and I travel with just this single piece." He motioned to the small leather chest that a footman, who was only now ascending the steps near them, carried.

Aunt Penny stared at the impossible size of the luggage and then took in the breadth of Sir Philip. In Muriel's estimation, an Exquisite such as the baronet would have needed a container at least ten times the size. Perhaps he only wore one set of clothing and the case contained only a selection of the many neckcloths he required.

"At once, madam," Huxley repeated, stepping away to make the needed arrangements.

"This is most excellent." Sir Philip, obviously pleased with the outcome, emanated cheer and goodwill. "I could not ask for more . . . Except, if I am to remain in your beautiful home, in your lovely company, would it be too much of an imposition to ask for a tour of the house and grounds at some later time?"

Bright-eyed Charlotte stepped forward, her lips parted, anxious to grant Sir Philip's request.

"My other niece, Lady Muriel's elder sister, Lady Charlotte." Aunt Penny gestured to Charlotte, who blinked, braved a smile at him, and sank into a curtsy.

"Ah, yes. The beautiful angel I've heard so much about," Sir Philip replied, turning his attention to her.

"How do you do?" As if Charlotte had planned it, a becoming flush of pink washed onto her cheeks, coming to full bloom once his attention was focused completely upon her.

No, this could not be.

Horrified at Charlotte's reaction, Muriel noticed an expression she had never seen upon her sister's face before. One of pure adoration . . . from her sister Charlotte . . . for Sir Philip Somerville?

No. No. No.

"How do you do? I am delighted to make your acquaintance," he said in quite another tone altogether.

Muriel laid a protective arm in front of Charlotte, preventing her from moving any closer in case Sir Philip should affect another extravagant display for her benefit.

Sir Philip did not repeat the ornate leg he had performed for her aunt. He reached out for Charlotte's hand and bowed over it with quiet intensity.

"I . . . I would be delighted to show you the grounds, if I might," Charlotte uttered when she found her voice.

Muriel simply could not believe what she saw. It was all too clear that Charlotte fancied this horrid, dreadful dandy.

Chapter Five

By the time Charlotte had come to her senses, she realized the recently arrived baronet, Sir Philip Somerville, had gone not only from her company but from the premises.

Aunt Penny had urged her nieces to accompany him to the stables and to assure him the transportation he needed was readily available. Muriel had wished him a lengthy journey to Bloxwich and an extended duration in the village that would detain him even longer. It seemed to Charlotte that her sister had taken somewhat of a dislike to him, although she could not imagine why.

Charlotte sighed. This gentleman had so impressed her with his exquisite manners and bearing. He had, after all, proclaimed himself an Exquisite, and she regarded him most favorably. She would not consider herself in love with his man. After all, she had only just made his acquaintance.

"Girls!" Aunt Penny called, directing their attention

to the road leading to their drive. "The first young man is just arriving now—with a pail in his hand."

"Oh, look—it is Sir Hugh!" Charlotte exclaimed. She had met Sir Hugh Linville only yesterday, but his constant smile and laughing eyes made sharing his company a delight. Whether his good humor was for show, Charlotte could not know.

"Is he not *very* handsome?" Muriel said, leaning against Charlotte to whisper and then laugh. "He certainly is a jolly one, that's for sure."

"And why shouldn't he be? He's the first to arrive," Aunt Penny said, wrapping an arm around each niece and, with modest pressure, urging them forward. "Let's greet him properly, shall we?"

They weren't the first to approach. A footman held the horse's head while Sir Hugh dismounted and handed his ante, a pail of ripe gooseberries, to one of the kitchen staff.

"Ladies!" Sir Hugh called upon seeing them approach. He brushed the sleeves of his jacket, made quick work of tugging at each glove for a snug fit, and removed his hat to properly greet them.

"Tell us, Sir Hugh, how did you do it?" Muriel's enthusiasm for the baronet was nearly equal to her delight in acquiring a new Latin textbook. "How did you manage to find so many ripe gooseberries so quickly?"

Sir Hugh glanced at Charlotte and his affable smile widened. "It was nothing really." He tried to shrug off his victory. She found that a touch of modesty suited him very well. "I simply sought out the spots of ripe berries from a distance while others crept tediously through the patch, searching willy-nilly for any fruit."

"How *clever* you are!" Muriel remarked, with an overabundance of brightness that was so very uncharacteristic of her when addressing any gentlemen. "Is he not clever, Charlotte?"

Muriel's curious behavior gave Charlotte pause. It was almost as if her sister were trying to create some interest on Sir Hugh's behalf.

"It is indeed quite an accomplishment," Charlotte agreed. "Come, we will proceed to the Blue Parlor, shall we? That is where we plan to take tea, is it not?"

"Tea will not be served for at least an hour yet," Aunt Penny reminded her niece. "The tarts and scones have yet to be baked. It such a nice day I thought we might sit outdoors. The east lawn perhaps. You must entertain Sir Hugh until our five other guests and Sir Nicholas arrive."

"And we are expecting Susan, Miss Wilbanks, as well," Muriel added to both Sir Hugh and Charlotte. "We cannot begin until all the guests are present."

"Yes, certainly." Charlotte had never observed this level of enthusiasm in her sister. "Do not concern yourselves, ladies. Sir Hugh and I will stroll very slowly, taking in the grounds and gardens on our way. I'm sure by the time we return to the house other guests will have joined us."

"An excellent suggestion. That is where the true reward lies." Sir Hugh must have immediately seen the benefit of being the first to acquire the berries.

"We shall point the other guests in your direction as they arrive," Aunt Penny informed them.

Muriel seemed pleased with the arrangement and added, "I shall join you as soon as I change into something more appropriate."

"Thank you, Aunt Penny." Charlotte could barely believe that her sister would make a genuine effort to be pleasant. It was so unlike Muriel, yet she could not bear to think ill of her sister. Charlotte stepped toward Sir Hugh, who offered her his arm. "Shall we begin?"

"By all means," Sir Hugh replied, leading her forward. "It would be my great pleasure."

With a saddle horse and the directions supplied by the Duke's stable boy, Philip trotted toward the local village of Bloxwich. The journey gave him time to ponder his morning. His small diversion might have begun as a minor detour with disastrous effects, but the incident was not completely objectionable. Yes, his curricle lay ruined and it was conceivable his London arrival would be a week late. No harm there; he simply would dash off a missive when he returned to Faraday Hall, informing his tailor to reschedule their appointment.

The manor itself held some interest. Not the building but its inhabitants, the three lovely ladies who welcomed Philip. The acquaintance of the elder sister, Lady Charlotte, was quite a pleasant surprise. Who'd expect to find such a rare beauty out here in the country? The thought of her put a smile on his face.

Philip arrived at the village and slowed his mount to

a walk. Although he had never set foot in this rural community, the main street felt crowded.

Adorned in the finest London style, a trio of young men lurked before a storefront. A pair of Corinthians across the way strolled in the opposite direction. Then he recalled the line of travelers he'd seen earlier. These men must have been Lady Charlotte's suitors.

"Oi, Sir Philip!" Donny Ellis, the kind local who had helped Philip only hours before, approached, hailing him.

"Good day to you." Philip halted his horse and dismounted to better converse.

"And to you, sir." Ellis doffed his hat. "Just come back from seein' Peter Strong now. I'll take you there if you like." He no longer needed to raise his voice to be heard.

"Again you come to my aid, Mr. Ellis. It is much appreciated."

"I take it Lady Muriel got you to Faraday all safe and sound, sir?" Ellis moved forward, gently leading the way.

"Yes, Lady Muriel did so with alacrity." Philip wondered how it came to be that her identity had not been immediately revealed by Ellis. "What news do you have for me, my man?"

"You'll not find your horses here in town." He gestured down the way. "There weren't no room. I've had your cattle stowed down at The Wild Rose; they can stay there until nightfall."

He would need to make further arrangements before the day's end. An inconvenience Philip would sort out once he had finished here.

"Sent young Sturgis ta fetch your rig first thing. He'll be bringin' it to Strong's straightaway. There be the shop." Ellis gestured to the left.

A man's rant rang out from the shop. "I've been waitin' for near-on a week, now!"

Ellis led Philip inside, where he caught sight of the outraged patron and a leather-aproned man, clearly Peter Strong. "That's Matthew Tyndale," Ellis whispered as a casual introduction.

"That be him right there. You blasted worm." Tyndale jabbed his large finger in their direction, pointing at Donny Ellis. "I heard what the two of you said. You can't just push my wagon aside 'cause some flush nob is havin' trouble gettin' to Town in time ta measure his swelled head for his new hat!"

Apparently news of Philip's disabled curricle had instigated the tirade. Subsequently his large cranium would be taking the brunt of the wrath—if not literally, then by earnest name-calling.

"That's right, been here waitin', my horse standin' idle; costs to feed him." Tyndale gestured wildly with his right arm. "An' what about me?" He pounded his chest. "I ain't worked since I made my last delivery—near a fortnight ago. What'll I do without my wagon? I got to make a livin'!"

"If you will excuse me, gentlemen." Philip interrupted before Strong could answer. "I believe there must be an amiable solution to our problem."

No, Philip certainly could not in all good conscience insist the wheelwright repair his curricle before this good man's wagon. He also did not wish to remain for a fortnight waiting for the repair of his vehicle and inconvenience the Duke and his family with his unexpected presence.

He had to find an agreeable solution for all their difficulties. Normally this type of situation was not difficult to solve. He felt he had only bits and pieces of a puzzle that when placed together in the correct sequence would set things to right. Currently he felt inexplicably distracted.

Somehow Philip needed to expedite the repair of his rig, find a solution to Mr. Tyndale's unemployment, and locate adequate lodging for his horses.

From the east lawn Muriel could easily see Charlotte and Sir Hugh pass before the maze. Susan Wilbanks joined them only moments after starting on the tour of the grounds.

Muriel had remained with Aunt Penny, who had donned a bonnet and busied herself directing the placement of tables and chairs.

Fifteen minutes after Sir Hugh's arrival, Lord Arthur Masters and Lord Irving appeared with their pails of gooseberries. The two men soon joined the company of Charlotte's group on their way toward the conservatory.

In another ten minutes, Sir Albert Stephenson, Mr. Chester Atwater, and Lord Paul Bancroft arrived, followed by Sir Nicholas.

Muriel thought it looked as though Mr. Atwater's and Lord Paul's jaws, now merely darkened bruises after the altercation in the assembly, were healing nicely. The thin scratches they sported on the sides of their faces were new. Upon second inspection, she noted that all of them seemed to have been afflicted with similar types of marks.

Muriel watched the visitors progress from the conservatory to the parterre.

"Sir Nicholas," Aunt Penny called to the baronet. "All went well, I trust?"

"Splendidly, ma'am." He removed his hat and bowed. "Good day to you, Lady Muriel."

"Sir Nicholas," Muriel returned. "I thank you for your help this morning."

"Think nothing of it. I am pleased to be of service."

"Now that you're here, I assume that all the guests have arrived? Shall we catch up to the others? I believe they have made their way to the pond by now." Aunt Penny gestured Sir Nicholas to the left.

"Your servant." Sir Nicholas offered her his arm and replaced his hat atop his head.

They caught up with the party, but Muriel was not there long before Susan pulled her aside.

"Look there, Moo." Susan nodded off toward the stables. "Is that he?"

They had not yet reached the pond. Muriel stared off to the left, watching the commotion of someone arriving at the stable. Sir Philip had returned.

"Do you think he might like to join us?" Susan sounded hopeful, but Muriel couldn't think of anything she dreaded more.

"Allow me to inquire," Muriel was quick to answer. She would do what she could to delay him, just in case the baronet should see them and get it into his head to spoil their private party.

Muriel excused herself, hoping she could come up with some way to keep Sir Philip occupied. At this moment, she could not envision how she would manage to detain him.

"Ah, young Lady Muriel!" Philip hailed, raising the top of his cane to greet her. He brushed at his sleeves, removing the travel dust he'd accumulated.

"Were you able to see to the repair of your transport?" she asked, strategically positioning herself with her back to the stables to prevent him from seeing the other guests.

"To my satisfaction, yes. The arrangements have been made. The completion will take a bit longer than I would have liked, but I shall not complain." Philip turned to the rear of the house and then to his left. He gauged the reason for her current position: to turn him away from the pond where he was fairly certain Charlotte's party would be visible.

"Would you care to see the gardens? The conservatory? The maze?" Muriel offered in quick succession.

Philip did not let on that he knew of her effort to keep him occupied. She must have felt a desperate need to keep him away from the festivities.

"You have a maze?" His eyebrows rose in curiosity. Another type of puzzle that never ceased to amuse him.

"It's a hedge maze. Allow me to show it to you. It's this way, please." Muriel led him down a path that led around the rear of the house.

"Might I ask the whereabouts of the rest of your family?" Philip had meant to upset her a bit, questioning her about a topic he knew she wished to avoid.

"Aunt Penny plans to serve tea on the east lawn," she answered without enthusiasm. "Some of the gentlemen who are staying in the village have been invited to join us."

"Ah, Lady Charlotte's suitors." He did his best to remain uninterested in the gentlemen suitors or in joining their gathering.

"Let us enter the Lapidarium. You'll have a better vantage point of the rear grounds." Muriel preceded him up the steps into the raised, covered outlook.

"This is indeed quite the collection of stones. Is it a natural outcropping?" Of course Philip understood the structure's literal Latin name. He followed her up the steps and admired the blending of the raised rock and man-made structure. "I find all this quite astonishing."

"Look there—at the maze corners. My father had the animal topiaries stationed at each of the entrances so we could tell them apart when we were very young children."

"Because only one beast must lead to the center. I can see as children you would have difficulty discerning which entrance would be the correct one."

"It's not quite that simple," she cautioned. "The paths are elaborate, but after years of practice we children could even make our way through the passages at night. Most people find it nearly impossible to navigate, even on the brightest of days."

"And yet the Duke's children managed to traverse this difficult maze." A smile touched Sir Philip's lips. "Your father, the Duke, is a very clever man."

"I believe you will have the pleasure of making his acquaintance. We expect Papa to return home in a day or two. It depends only on how quickly he is able to leave Parliament."

"Sits in the House of Lords, does he?"

Muriel nodded.

"Quite commendable. I, too, plan to take my place when my time comes. My father can't be bothered to attend. It's inexcusable, if you ask me." He may have shown his parent in an unflattering light, but Philip would voice his opinion. "People depend upon him and he shirks his duty simply because he . . . chooses not to assume the responsibility. When one is in a position of influence, one must do what one can to promote conditions for those who cannot."

"Well said, sir," she agreed.

"What other structures of note are there at Faraday Hall? Did we or did we not pass an orangery adjacent to the conservatory on our way here?"

"We did."

"Had you planned for us to inspect that as well?"

"I was hoping you would insist."

"I do. Now let us be on our way." Philip stepped to the ground and raised his hand to aid her descent.

Muriel hesitated for a few moments but then accepted his gesture. Her refined conduct was a far cry from the

country girl he had first thought her when they met earlier that day.

"Do not think I have not noticed," he said, surrepti-
tiously admiring her beneath his lowered lids. "You are
quite the lady in that frock."

"Is that an actual compliment? For me?" She glanced
up to him when stepping upon the ground. "I'm afraid
your pretty sentiments fall upon deaf ears."

"That cannot be."

"I'm afraid so. I am certain I would ruin your day by
admitting that not everyone dresses at the height of fashion on a daily basis."

"Are you referring to yourself? That would be a shame.
When your time comes to marry, I daresay you shall be
quite as breathtaking as your sister." His attention drifted
into the distance, in the direction of the pond and Charlotte. He paid no mind to his companion's reaction.

"I take it you would like to join our other guests?"
Muriel studied him, gauging his interest.

"For tea, yes. I'm afraid that I am not, as of yet, ready
for a wife." Philip knew that someday he must do his
duty—marry and provide for the future of his family
line. It was a step he would not take lightly. "A lovely
face is often enough found, but what I require is more. I
must find a woman with whom I can share more than
occasional polite words. Do not mistake me, young lady.
I find your sister very lovely indeed."

Muriel gazed heavenward; clearly she was tolerating
his lengthy discourse.

"It takes far more than mere beauty, I dare say. Your sister may be perfection itself in one respect, but I cannot vouch for her other qualities," he told her truthfully. "It has been my experience that young women who have the extreme beauty your sister possesses have characters that I consider somewhat . . . lacking."

Muriel might have been insulted on her sister's behalf if she were not so overjoyed at his declaration. She need not worry that he should try to infiltrate her family by marriage.

"You do not wish to marry a beautiful lady?" Muriel found herself curious about his requirements for a wife. What did Sir Philip think important?

"I shall not complain, mind you, but beauty is not everything, not even the most important quality. Those types of women rely primarily on their appearance instead of substance to achieve their goals. Thus, as they grow into mature womanhood, they become selfish, self-centered, and vain."

To lump any and all pretty girls into a single category and chastise them all? The man is too hateful!

"I expect a wife to be not only accomplished in music and the arts but, above all, in possession of a large quantity of compassion."

Muriel stared at him, thinking she had never come across this sort of man before. She thought him quite unusual, but still completely unlikable.

"Will you take your place in Parliament when your time comes? You seem occupied with . . . *other* interests." Should she have noted them by name? He was an out-

and-out dandified, pompous fop who thought himself better than he ought.

"Most certainly. I shall not shirk my duty and the great responsibility that comes with inheriting my title." A pained expression crossed his normally placid visage. "Ah, it so happens, I am only a peer by chance of birth and an Exquisite by endeavor."

And he brags about it!

"Self-improvement is achievable by anyone," Sir Philip informed her, "no matter what social position, and appreciated by all."

Coming to the corner of the conservatory, Muriel stopped. Thank goodness they'd arrived. Perhaps stepping inside the glass structure and gazing upon the various botanical specimens might distract him from the topic of himself. Muriel would not have been surprised to discover the baronet a self-proclaimed botany expert.

"Look there." Sir Philip extended his walking stick in the direction of a small gathering, mainly of men, strolling toward the pond that lay at the far edge of the property. Easily identified even from this distance—Charlotte in her blue gown, Susan in her peach frock, and Aunt Penny in her lavender skirt—the three women trailed across the green that lay on the far side of Faraday Hall.

"So those men are Lady Charlotte's suitors?" Sir Philip mused. He tapped the handle of his cane against his chin in thought and chuckled softly.

His pleased reaction was the single quality Muriel found pleasurable.

"The notion that I should wish to marry her is folly."

Muriel was more than delighted to hear she had over-estimated his interest. Then again, he was not well acquainted with her sister. He had, without knowing, described the kindhearted Charlotte perfectly, down to her last compassionate attribute.

She played the pianoforte and the harp with equal proficiency. Her voice was an instrument without compare, perfection itself, as was her skill in watercolor, sketching, drawing, embroidery, and sewing. She spoke French and Italian fluently. As for compassion, Charlotte possessed this quality, too much of it, some people would say—a detail Sir Philip must never discover.

Sir Philip could not know Charlotte possessed everything he wished for in a wife. Muriel decided he may believe he was not interested in her sister, but if he were to learn of the real Charlotte, he might change his mind about competing for her hand.

Muriel took it upon herself to ensure he would never be in a position to find out. She vowed she would do all she could to keep Sir Philip and her sister apart.

Chapter Six

Charlotte could not believe how Muriel stepped right in front of Lord Paul. The poor man lifted his hand, guarding his bruised face in case it should be accidentally harmed.

"I beg that you excuse me, Lord Paul. I need a moment with Charlotte," Muriel interrupted, and whispered to her sister, "A word with you, Char-Char. It is most important."

A quick glance at the other guests sitting in a comfortable circle told Charlotte they had not been alarmed by her sister's impertinent behavior.

Muriel led her from the guests, rather forcefully, Charlotte thought.

"I could not keep Sir Philip from wishing to join our party," Muriel said, sounding rather displeased.

"That is understandable." Charlotte did not think the baronet would like to have been kept from the festivities. "He is our houseguest. Why should we not include him?"

"There is no good reason, I suppose, but that is not why I wish to speak to you." There was a gleam in Muriel's eye, the sort of expression she acquired when she had a particularly brilliant and, sometimes, questionable idea.

"What is it, Moo?" Charlotte was anxious to hear, not out of pure curiosity, but in the case it should prove particularly unpleasant, she might be able to discourage her sister.

Muriel drew Charlotte from the lawn area and into the Oriental Room, closing the door firmly behind them. "I thought perhaps we could use this opportunity to your advantage, to further test the gentlemen's affection and devotion to you."

"Do you not think they have been through enough, Moo? Only look at them—scraped and bruised." Charlotte did not wish to bring up their guests' self-inflicted injuries from the previous evening. "They need cold compresses, not a prodding to risk further injury."

"Has it ever occurred to you that all those gentlemen desire you for your perfection? What if you were not as wonderful as they believe? What if you had something hideously wrong with you, an unseen abnormality perhaps. They would run from Faraday Hall, from Bloxwich, from Essex completely!"

"I do not have such a thing." Charlotte did not think so, anyway.

"It needn't be true. It would be something we would make up. I was thinking the winner of this new contest could learn a bit about you. Something personal, private, to better know you. The gentlemen may think it would improve their standing."

"Is that not too cruel?" Charlotte could never have come up with a ruse such as this, but her sister might prove correct, as she often had.

"You could have something such as . . ." Muriel paused for a few moments and glanced about the room as though searching for an answer. "Your eye."

"Is there something wrong with my eyes?" Charlotte stared at her sister with the left orb and moved the right one, in a jiggling motion, toward the door, and then laughed at her trick. It never failed to disturb Augusta.

"Yes, that's exactly it!" Muriel laughed, with Charlotte joining her. "You'll tell them it wanders!"

"A wandering eye?" Charlotte squinted at her sister, not completely understanding. "That is not so very bad. An unpleasant trait in a wife, I would think."

"Don't you see? You invent a flaw for yourself, and then you'll see how much those gentlemen truly care for you—wayward eye and all."

"Moo, that is famous!" Charlotte leaped up and clapped her hands. Her excitement ebbed and she quieted. "What if it should frighten them all away?"

"Then they do not truly care for you. Have no fear, Char-Char. I'm sure it will take more than a wandering eye to put them off. If you feel so guilty about it, you could offset the bad news with a bit of good."

"In the same vein as gooseberries are my favorite

berry . . . I could tell them my favorite color, flower, or food?" It would be just like sweet Charlotte to focus on how this would benefit one lucky young man and not on how the news might disappoint the many who would find her seemingly less-than-perfect eye unacceptable.

"That's right." Muriel knew differently. She did not expect the rumors they were about to start to have a positive effect.

"Who shall I tell first?"

"Well . . . it is my opinion that free knowledge is worth little value. You must make them *work* for it."

"Work? Another challenge, perhaps?"

"Yes, exactly." Muriel stepped farther back into the room, away from the floor-to-ceiling windows.

"What do you think about a footrace?" Charlotte suggested.

Muriel paused, rethinking her sister's idea. "Do you expect all those men to dash across the lawn?"

"You must admit physical competition does have merit." But Charlotte considered what the gentlemen had already been through. "Is it too much to ask from them, do you think?"

"The offer of an unappealing bit of information will test their commitment." Muriel clasped Charlotte's clenched hand, begging her to understand. "Just think how happy it will make whoever is left to learn your eye does not wander. That you are as perfect as he first imagined."

"I would think it might anger him."

"He won't be angry; he'll be grateful. All the others

will have been driven away, and you will have managed to prove he is as devoted to you as one could be." Muriel blinked up at her sister. "What do you say, Char-Char? Is the contest on?"

Charlotte wasn't sure what to do. But certainly something had to be done, for there were too many suitors and she had no idea how to lessen their number. Should she go along with Muriel's plan?

"Very well, Moo," Charlotte replied. "Let's inform the men they should assemble at the starting line."

It wasn't a surprise to Muriel that all six gentlemen were willing and anxious participants in the contest. As soon as Charlotte had put forth the idea, there was no stopping it from happening. The men shed their jackets and unbuttoned their waistcoats or removed them altogether, putting Charlotte and Susan to the blush.

"You mean they are to run a common footrace?" Whether Aunt Penny was more outraged or shocked was difficult to tell. "I have never seen such a thing in my entire life. How has this simple tea party gotten out of hand? We've lost any amount of respectability it might have had."

"Don't go on so, Auntie," Muriel said, trying to reassure her. "It's just a good bit of fun."

Stepping away from her aunt, Muriel moved closer to Charlotte and Susan, who stood to one side of the starting line in front of the men.

Their shirtsleeves had been ripped, torn by the gooseberry thorns, and were spotted with blood where they'd been deeply scratched. There was further embarrassment when they removed their gloves. Barely healed scratches crisscrossed the length of their hands and forearms. It must have been painful, but not a single man uttered a complaint.

Standing off to the other side, Sir Nicholas was probably making a last-minute wager with Lord Paul and Mr. Atwater. If the Duke ever discovered this disgrace, there was no telling how long Sir Nicholas' exile would last this time.

Finally, Sir Nicholas took his place, raised his arm, and held a small pistol in the air. "On your marks!" he shouted to the line of gentlemen in various states of undress. "Ready . . ."

Muriel drew in a breath. Lord Stanton, Lord Irving, and Sir Hugh had removed their boots, having every intention of realizing victory in their stocking feet.

"Steady . . ."

Muriel held her breath as Charlotte and Susan must have—not a sound came from them. Sir Albert, Mr. Atwater, and Lord Paul adjusted their foot positions in preparation of the start.

"GO!" Sir Nicholas pulled the trigger, sending a shot into the air and signaling the beginning of the race. The six men sprinted across the great lawn, stretching from the parterre to the walkway of the conservatory where members of the household staff would witness the first to cross the imaginary finish line.

"You cannot expect these men to dash about as if they were racehorses," said Aunt Penny, but her disapproval came far too late. The gentlemen thought the opportunity to learn something personal about Charlotte, or so it was announced, was well worth the effort.

Lord Irving threw his fists into the air in victory, crossing the finish line first. Charlotte, Muriel, and Susan cheered.

Sir Philip appeared next to the three after the thundering suitors had charged past him. He was immaculately dressed, looking so much more elegant compared to the coatless, gloveless, and bootless men.

"I believe I have missed something rather important." Sir Philip came around from the far side of Aunt Penny, straining to see the once thundering herd.

"I don't know if it was important, but it was all rather exciting, I must say," she confessed.

"It was a fantastic display of physical exertion, Mrs. Parker!" Sir Philip replied. "Quite invigorating." He huffed and thumped his green paisley brocade-covered chest and then splayed his hand over the material. "Viscount Irving has dashed across the finish line, and I expect there is a worthwhile prize for his victory."

"Yes, I believe there must be," she confirmed.

The participants gathered, puffing hard with their recent exertion. Lord Irving laughed between labored gasps of air.

Charlotte greeted her champion. "Lord Irving, when you are ready, I await your arm, if you please."

Lord Irving retrieved his clothing. He unrolled his sleeves, pulled on his boots, and shrugged into his jacket, making himself presentable. Still breathing heavily from the exertion of the race, he accompanied Charlotte to the parterre to receive his well-earned prize.

He smiled, eyes wide, anxious for his reward. Charlotte settled onto the stone bench and glanced up at him. "Lord Irving?"

"Yes, Lady Charlotte?" He brushed the dust from his breeches and adjusted his gloves after slipping them on.

"I have two bits of personal information for you." Charlotte felt her face warm and glanced away. Whether it was because she felt self-conscious about revealing something personal to a near stranger or because she was about to relay a bouncer, she could not be certain. "Lord Irving, I have something to tell you."

"Yes, Lady Charlotte." Lord Irving smiled, leaning the slightest bit forward in anticipation.

"A pleasant item." She smiled and tried to hold the expression steady. *And one bit of unpleasant news.* "Please, Lord Irving." Her throat tightened, making speech difficult. She felt certain her problem was due to the untruth that was about to pass through her trembling lips.

"Lady Charlotte." He held her hand fast in a firm grip once again. "I beg of you, if such an admission causes you discomfort, I suggest you do not—"

"No, no . . . I must continue. I promised. Your victory has earned you the privilege."

Lord Irving gazed at her expectantly, eager to have an advantage over the other gentlemen.

"I do not believe the news will be agreeable to you."

She then suspected that Muriel had intended that to be the outcome from the start. Still, it did not please Charlotte to disclose information that might be considered disturbing.

"Lady Charlotte," he whispered, moving closer until he finally sat next to her on the stone bench. "I do not believe there is anything about you that one could possibly find disagreeable."

The tension in her shoulders relaxed at his words, and she smiled. It was very kind of him to make her feel at ease.

"Please, I beg that you continue. Nothing about you could ever displease me."

"Very well." Charlotte cleared her throat. "Lord Irving, I have two items to divulge about myself. One, both, or neither may benefit you." He remained quiet and appeared eager to hear more. "Lord Irving, my right eye . . . has a tendency to wander."

"W-wander, you say?" He did not exactly back away from her at the discovery, but he did seem to stare at her more pointedly.

Charlotte prepared to perform her eye trick as she had so many times for her siblings and stared at the yew over his shoulder, allowing her right eye to pull to the side.

He jerked back from her with every twitch of her eye. "The eye is c-completely f-false, isn't it?"

Noting the expected, horrified response Muriel had anticipated, Charlotte felt quite dreadful for her deception. Tears moistened her eyes at her disappointment at his reaction.

"H-how long have you . . . ?" He stood and brought his hand to his chin as he considered what he had just seen. "Never mind."

"Lord Irving, I—" Charlotte discovered that he could no longer face her.

"I think it time that I must be going." He straightened and still could not address her directly. He bowed and said, "Good day to you, my lady."

"My lord, I have yet to tell you the other item. The good bit." Silence ensued as he passed the stone bench to take his leave.

Charlotte called out to his retreating form, "My favorite color is robin egg blue."

"I believe Lord Irving has left Faraday Hall," Muriel informed her sister. She found Charlotte sitting on the stone bench alone. Her hands were clasped, resting in her lap, and her head was lowered in sorrow.

"I have hurt him. I know it." Charlotte would never have cried for herself. She always wept for others, for their loss or their pain, but never her own.

"What do you care? He has fled at the prospect of your blemish. An imperfection that is imaginary."

"It must have disturbed him greatly." Charlotte sniffed, regretting that she had ever listened to her sister. "It was terrible. Lord Irving could not rid himself of my presence quickly enough. You should have seen his face. His expression was . . . He appeared quite mortified.

"I told him my eye wandered. Why did he leap to the

conclusion that it was false?" Emotion threatened to choke her words. "Of course that would frighten him, it would frighten anyone. I believe it was most unkind of me to tell him such a thing, Moo."

"It is not your fault he chose to exaggerate your tale."

"I suppose that is true." Charlotte sighed. "What if he should tell the other gentlemen?"

"It would be the best possible outcome imaginable, Char-Char. The more who know, the more we can be certain of their true affection. The ones who do not return did not truly care for you."

"Why must you see the worst in people?" This wasn't the first time she'd chastised Muriel for her suspicious nature.

"I might ask you why you always see the good in everyone," Muriel countered.

"Whether you wish to see it or not, most people are good and kind. If given a proper chance, that is," Charlotte added in an afterthought. "If you were older than fifteen, you might see that for yourself. Now, if you will excuse me, I have other guests."

Charlotte walked away as calmly as if she had not just had a row with her sister. Muriel headed along the side of the house. She waved at Susan, who, it seemed, was the last remaining person standing on the east lawn, along with a few servants.

"They've gone," Susan told Muriel when she came within conversational range. "Every one of them."

"All of them?" Muriel glanced toward the rear terrace

and then the stables. There was no one in sight. Had Lord Irving's hasty exit precipitated the other gentlemen's departure?

"It was quite amazing really." Susan brushed Muriel's arm and nodded to a man walking up the drive. "Do you think that might be one gentleman who's changed his mind?"

"Let us see, shall we?" Muriel linked her arm through her friend's, and together they walked toward the drive to welcome their visitor. It did not take long to see it was not a young man in fine dress, but a middle-aged one in rather worn clothing. Muriel soon recognized Mr. Ellis.

"Good day to you, Lady Muriel, Miss Susan." He removed his hat, greeting them, and appeared in very high spirits.

"Greetings, Mr. Ellis," Susan replied.

Muriel nodded her head, acknowledging him.

"I'm here to speak to Sir Philip Somerville. Would you happen to know if he's about?" Mr. Ellis glanced around as he spoke.

"Did he not pay you as he said he would?" Muriel would not find this a surprise. She tried not to smile or appear too cheery at this dreadful news.

"Paid me for my trouble, he did. More than enough." Mr. Ellis smiled, replacing his hat. "Just need to tell him I'd brought his cattle to ole Gilbert's farm, like he told me."

"Sir Philip's horses?" The reference startled Muriel from her disappointment at the baronet settling his accounts in a timely manner. "The pair of bays that pulled his curricle?"

"Aye, that be his cattle, alright." Mr. Ellis laughed.

"Why would he do that?" Susan seemed puzzled by the action. "Have them brought to the village, and then have them brought all the way to Farmer Gilbert's?"

"Put them on a bloomin' holiday, he does. Treats them like royalty." Mr. Ellis rubbed his jaw.

Muriel motioned for them to proceed to the manor. "Let us speak to Huxley regarding the baronet's whereabouts."

Sir Philip showing kindness to his horses almost made him likable, but Muriel could still not bring herself to think of him in any way nice.

"Had me order new traces, as well. Old ones were roughed up some, but not torn through or any such thin', didn't need to bother," Mr. Ellis continued. "Eli Hubbard were glad to have the work, I tell you. I think Sir Philip single-handedly brought more business to the village than the lot of young London swells."

Susan brightened and announced, "Just imagine that—Sir Philip making everyone happy!"

Not exactly everyone, Muriel added silently to herself.

Chapter Seven

Muriel glanced at Sir Philip just as he laid his fork and knife upon his empty plate. Because of his company, supper had been a bit more formal than the previous evening when only the three ladies attended.

Sir Philip sat to the right of the Duke's place setting at the head of the table, now empty. The baronet had changed from his brown frock coat and buckskins into an exquisitely cut blue superfine, buff trousers, and a decidedly crisp cravat tied with perfection.

Charlotte, in one of her favorite muted blue gowns, sat to the baronet's right. Muriel, who had allowed her sister to advise her on what was proper to be worn, sat across from Sir Philip, and Penny sat to Muriel's left.

"I think watching the footrace this afternoon has given me quite an appetite." Sir Philip pressed his napkin to his mouth before folding it at the conclusion of the meal.

He must have noticed the gentlemen's cravats were a conglomeration of limp and wilted linens by the end of the race. The very thought of it might have been too much for someone of Sir Philip's delicate dressing sensibilities.

"I did not think I could manage to finish a single course." He folded his napkin and laid it next to his plate.

"What a surprise," Muriel mumbled. "He is capable of thought—or so he says."

Aunt Penny nudged Muriel under the table with her foot but did not alert the others by looking at her youngest niece.

"I hope you found the meal satisfactory, sir." Charlotte's food had remained virtually untouched, not that she had placed much on her plate to begin with. Apparently the day's activity must have affected her appetite as well.

Aunt Penny gestured to a footman that it was time for Sir Philip's port.

"It has been quite a day—with the accident, attending to the repairs, and the footrace." Sir Philip chuckled at the recollection.

"Gracious—it's a wonder you've managed to recover enough to dine with us," Muriel added in a murmur. She could not sit by and keep her disagreeable opinions to herself.

"Enough!" Aunt Penny grunted under her breath. She swung her foot a bit more forcefully toward Muriel's leg, this second attempt successfully hitting the mark.

Muriel did not react and shifted her legs out of her aunt's reach, lest a third attempt should be made.

"What entertainment do you have planned for to-morrow, ladies, if I may ask?" Sir Philip looked at each of them for an answer. "I fear for the gentlemen's accessories—hats, fobs, and walking sticks."

They had not discussed the following day. Surely they could expect callers, many more than the six who had won coveted spots for tea, but far fewer than the previous day's.

"Sir Philip?" Muriel called to him, in a voice half an octave higher than normal. "Do you plan to visit Blox-wich on business tomorrow? I believe you said some-thing about the need to find a valet."

"And so I do." He accepted his after-dinner drink from the footman and raised his glass to Muriel.

"We shall leave you to your port, sir," said Aunt Penny. "If you will excuse us." She moved from the table, as did her nieces, who followed her out of the din-ing room.

Moving down the corridor, Aunt Penny encouraged Charlotte to enter the Citrus Parlor first. It was the room where a cozy fire in the hearth awaited them, where they spent most evenings plying their embroidery needle or reading.

With a hand on Muriel's shoulder, Aunt Penny delayed her. "A word, if you please."

Muriel slowed and stopped at the threshold. She re-mained silent.

"I am outraged at your conduct toward our guest," Aunt Penny scolded her. "I'm sure he has done nothing to warrant your harsh words."

"He is after our Charlotte." Muriel directed a stern gaze at her aunt.

"Oh, tish-tosh! He has not shown the least bit of interest in her."

"This aloof man-about-town is not to be trusted. He is not what he seems," Muriel told her aunt. "He is very careful in showing his true self to others, for good reason, but he does not fool me."

"Perhaps His Grace is correct in believing you need a governess. Perhaps a ladies' school for manners would not be out of the question." To threaten Muriel with the mundane had always convinced her to mend her ways, only in this instance it may not have been a threat. "You will pay Sir Philip the respect that he is due, am I understood?"

"Completely, Aunt Penny." Muriel moved forward to take her embroidery from her sister. "Thank you, Char-Char."

"Moo, I am convinced that you could improve if only you would put your mind to it." Charlotte spoke regarding her embroidery skills, not her manners. "Here's your hoop, Aunt Penny."

"You sister is capable of a great many things, Char, but only when she is genuinely determined."

"Was he not handsome this evening?" Charlotte sank onto the sofa but did not move to ply her needle. "His dark blue jacket was certainly flattering, as was his cravat; it took a skilled hand to—" Her eyebrows rose in either confusion or comprehension. "He does not employ a valet, did you say, Moo?"

"For goodness' sake, enough about our guest, if you please." Muriel huffed, seating herself on the opposite end of the sofa. "Aunt Penny, do you have any notion what we should plan for tomorrow afternoon?"

"We should have something in mind, surely." Aunt Penny eased into the overstuffed chair decorated with bright yellow lemons. "There must be some diversion for the gentlemen who come to call. A display of Charlotte's talent would be . . . some music, perhaps?"

"We could certainly play several duets," Muriel said, suddenly caught up with her aunt's idea. "And I'm sure Sukey would join our party if she were asked; she has forever been practicing with us."

"We'll also need Sir Nicholas to spread the word to the gentlemen," Aunt Penny added. She would plead for his help yet again.

"Right this way, sir." Huxley's familiar voice alerted the three they would soon have company.

Muriel, Charlotte, and Aunt Penny straightened in their seats. A shuffling of skirts and an exchange of glances passed among them before Sir Philip stepped into the room. The three stood as he entered.

"I beg your pardon—I do not wish to disturb you." He motioned for them not to rise, but it was too late. "Please do not bother yourselves."

"It is nothing, only a ladies' occupation." Aunt Penny gestured for him to be seated and eased back into her chair, as did Muriel, gathering up their embroidery now that they had company.

"A worthwhile lady's endeavor," Sir Philip said. "Would you mind showing me your efforts?"

"I attempt to make improvements," said Charlotte, reaching back to retrieve her hoop. Muriel came to her aid, substituting her own instead. "I believe one should continually improve upon one's craft."

"Is this"—he glanced upon the stitching with a certain bit of bewilderment—"your fine handiwork?" The marked surprise on Sir Philip's face could not be masked.

How did Charlotte not realize he gazed upon the wrong hoop? Muriel was certain her sister's singular thought was for the baronet and that she saw nothing else.

"Quite commendable, indeed." Sir Philip cleared his throat, obviously pushing aside all honesty. "I admire your determination."

Muriel stood, retrieving the hoop, and put all of them into the basket. "Excuse me, I need to write Sukey regarding tomorrow afternoon."

"I also need to pen a missive at once." Aunt Penny rose and moved to the drop-front secrétaire. "Will you have the Music Room lit for our inspection?"

"Yes, Aunt Penny," Muriel said before stepping from the room. "I shall return momentarily."

Charlotte would be left to entertain Sir Philip, if only for the few minutes it would take to write Sir Nicholas.

"Would you care to take a turn about the room, Sir Philip?" Charlotte offered, being the sole idle family member.

Even though the room was small and the stroll along

the perimeter would take no time at all, Charlotte had done the proper thing by making the suggestion to occupy their guest.

Charlotte nearly shivered in anticipation when she placed her hand upon Sir Philip's arm, accepting his escort. Their contact, although not intimate, excited her beyond belief. How could he not feel something between them?

"This panel on this Sèvres was the inspiration for this room." She motioned to the decorative vase. "Papa had this small parlor decorated with various types of citrus. When we discovered these plates depicting lemons and limes, we added them to our collection."

"And that is the reason this parlor has the most delectable depictions of these fruits," Sir Philip added.

"Exactly." Why it pleased her that he could see their reasons for creating their parlor, she did not know, but it had.

Sir Philip glanced about. His gaze followed the twining vinelike motif that curled its way along the upper edge of the wall near the ceiling. His preoccupation gave Charlotte time to admire him.

"Enchanting," he proclaimed. "Quite enchanting."

Sir Philip must not have cared for her at all. The very thought saddened her. Any one of her current suitors would have been exceedingly pleased to be in Sir Philip's place.

Clearly Sir Philip was only being polite and did not wish to further his acquaintance with Charlotte. He must have thought of her as the daughter of his absent host, and beyond that, nothing more.

How she wished there was a spark in his eyes when he looked at her, some gaiety in his voice when addressing her. How could Charlotte feel as if she would burst with joy when by his side while he, Sir Philip, remained oblivious to her interest?

Philip caught a glimpse of Lady Charlotte's exquisite profile. In that moment he realized exactly how much beauty she possessed. A type of beauty rarely seen even in the most elegant ballrooms of London.

He felt his face suffuse with an uncomfortable warmth, and his cravat felt as if it grew snugger by the second. The realization astounded him and he quickly consoled himself by amending that an admission of her beauty was not a declaration of any sort of affection.

She was merely an exceptionally lovely lady. There was no harm admitting such. It was, after all, common knowledge in this household.

"I have sent a note off to Yewhill Grange," Muriel announced, returning to the Citrus Parlor. "And the Music Room has been lit."

Charlotte and Philip stopped to regard Lady Muriel. "We have asked Miss Wilbanks to accompany us on the pianoforte tomorrow afternoon," Charlotte informed him with a vibrancy in her voice that told of her excitement.

"Is there to be a musical recital tomorrow for your gentlemen callers?" Philip regretted he would not be able to attend. He already had plans for the following afternoon. "How delightful!"

"Why don't you proceed to the Music Room?" Mrs. Parker suggested. "I have nearly finished here."

"If you would do me the honor, Lady Muriel," Philip said, offering her his other arm.

Muriel refused politely and tendered a compromise of her own. "I shall lead the way."

"Tell me more what you have planned for tomorrow." Philip sounded as if he were genuinely interested.

"We shall play Mozart," Charlotte began, "a Vivaldi piece, and that nice Bach sonata we all love. You know the one, Moo—I mean Muriel."

"I know the very one," Muriel replied, pushing the double doors open wide.

Inside the Music Room, the wall sconces burned brightly, illumining the coffered ceiling and decorative friezes. Philip turned toward the front of the room where the harp and pianoforte sat. Behind them a collection of polished, stringed instruments and shiny horns of various shapes and sizes lined the wall.

"And what is it you play?" he murmured to Charlotte. He held up his hand, halting her reply. "No other instrument except the harp would do you justice, I think."

"You are so very clever, Sir Philip," Charlotte replied, smiling at his veiled compliment.

Philip's gaze moved to Muriel. "I expect the devil's own violin would suit you best." Oh, how it brought him such pleasure to tease her.

"My violin skills do not match our sister Augusta's."

Muriel displayed a tight smile and remained civil. "I shall play the flute."

"Ah, you own to Pan's talent," Philip replied with true understanding. "The ability to inspire disorder and fear."

Chapter Eight

Muriel looked up from her book when movement at the doorway of the Breakfast Parlor caught her eye. "Good morning, Aunt Penny," she said, with Charlotte repeating the same only moments later.

"Good morning, girls." Aunt Penny shuffled through the morning post. Her hands didn't exactly shake, but there was a perceivable tension in the unsteady manner with which she sorted through the correspondence. "I think we may have moved forward with our afternoon with too much haste. There have been too many rushed missives, allowing the possibility of erroneous communication. I fear the sheer number of guests that might land on our doorstep."

If, indeed, any gentlemen had decided to return after hearing of Charlotte's wayward eye, it would be remarkable. Muriel fully expected Lord Irving to have spread the tale by this time.

"I fear the situation could get out of hand again," continued Aunt Penny. "I cannot have another footrace taking place. Such things will surely cause a scandal!" She returned to the correspondence in her hands.

"Allow me to fetch you some coffee, Aunt Penny," Charlotte said, rising from the table and proceeding to the sideboard.

"Thank you." She handed the first missive to Muriel and simply said, "Eton." It was merely a remark, not a commentary on Muriel's ongoing dispute with the educational establishment. "Do you still petition the Head Master for acceptance?"

Muriel did not wish to hear how futile her effort was. Glancing at the handwriting, she knew exactly who had penned this latest reply.

"It is her dearest wish to further her studies, Aunt Penny," said Charlotte, placing a cup of coffee at Aunt Penny's customary place at the table and returning to her own seat. "I applaud her effort."

Muriel placed the letter on the table, ignoring it for the time being. It was better left to be read in private.

"A letter from Augusta!" Aunt Penny announced, handing it to Charlotte, who happily accepted it. "Will you read this for us?"

Charlotte took her time opening her sister's letter, while remaining attentive to the undisclosed correspondences.

"This is from His Grace." It was an answer to Aunt Penny's missive of the day before. She glanced at her nieces. They were all anxious to hear what the Duke had to say. "Thank goodness. Perhaps he will know what to do better than our day-to-day conjecture."

"How could we possibly have made adequate arrangements?" Muriel complained. "It's not as if we had any warning they were about to descend upon us en masse."

"Aunt Penny is doing the best she can, Moo." Charlotte defended their aunt unnecessarily. "We all are."

"Please, let us not start bickering among ourselves, shall we?" Aunt Penny straightened the missive and began to read. "He writes, *If Faraday Hall is expected to host the majority of the Season's population, regardless if we are pleased to do so or not, we must provide proper diversions.*"

"I suppose we must continue to do what we can until he arrives," Charlotte said, sounding as cautious as Aunt Penny had.

Aunt Penny scanned the end of the missive and then paraphrased his remaining thoughts. "His Grace will conclude his business and return home as soon as it is feasible. He expects to arrive sometime today, perhaps tomorrow at the latest." She passed the letter to Charlotte, to allow her to read her father's words for herself.

The remaining correspondence was an invitation to a ball given by Lord and Lady Hopkins for their daughter Lady Margaret tomorrow evening at The Acorns.

"A ball?" Charlotte could not have sounded more delighted at the news.

"But had they not gone to London months ago?" Muriel was clearly confused by their change in circumstance. How could the Hopkins possible give a party here in the country? "Margaret was to attend the Season this year."

"Apparently they have returned," Aunt Penny stated.

"Obviously." Muriel resigned herself to her plight—her presence would prove unavoidable.

"Dust off your dancing slippers, Moo," Aunt Penny alerted her. "With the number of gentlemen who will no doubt attend, you will not have cause to sit out a single set."

"We need not plan an activity for tomorrow since we shall all enjoy an evening of dancing." Charlotte's eyes sparkled with delight. "How wonderful for all of us!"

"How wonderful, indeed," Muriel groaned, not pleased in the least.

"I shall wear Mama's string of pearls," Charlotte said at once and then added, "No, it will not do. Perhaps my topaz cross?" She placed her hand at her throat as if envisioning her precious necklace.

Muriel remained silent, merely moving her tolerant gaze away from her beloved sibling.

The news brought a much-needed smile to Aunt Penny's lips. It must have pleased her that Charlotte would have a night where she could wholly enjoy herself, since she had been denied her Season.

"I can wear one of my new gowns," Charlotte continued, oblivious to her sister's disinterest in her fashionable wardrobe. "The silver-shot lutestring—I think that should look very nice."

Charlotte probably hadn't the slightest notion of Muriel's dislike for parties. In Muriel's opinion, there were too many people to tolerate and it took too much effort to behave agreeably.

Unfortunately, Aunt Penny was probably correct. There

would be no sitting or standing at the edge of the dance floor with the number of young men who had recently arrived.

There is nothing I detest more than dancing, thought Muriel.

Muriel left the Breakfast Parlor and came upon Susan Wilbanks just entering the manor. She had finished removing her bonnet and cloak, leaving them in the care of a footman.

"Please tell me we are to practice before our performance." Susan wrung her hands, either with worry or to simply limber her fingers before sitting at the keyboard.

"Do not worry, Sukey," Muriel assured her friend. "You could play before a filled theater, for you are always perfection itself upon the pianoforte."

"Always? When we play for only ourselves, yes." Susan concerned herself over nothing. "However, my fingers may fumble upon the first attempt at Vivaldi."

"Char-Char wishes to rehearse as well." Muriel motioned for Susan to follow her up the stairs. "I expect we have less than three hours before our first guest appears."

"*Less* than three hours?" Susan's excitement was palpable. "Let us collect Char-Char and begin at once!"

"Gracious, Sukey, calm yourself." Muriel glared at her friend in a stern manner. "Lydia is dressing Char-Char now and it will take me only a moment to don my frock. You can help me with my tapes."

Upon seeing Susan's dress choice, Muriel changed

into a dissimilar green sprig muslin to complement the Pomona green day gown Charlotte planned to wear.

Some time later, Muriel and Susan met with Charlotte in the Music Room. They played each piece to their satisfaction. Aunt Penny suggested the girls move to the Citrus Parlor to relax before the gentlemen's arrival.

Twenty minutes later Aunt Penny appeared at the doorway and announced, "It is time." Muriel detected some anxiety in her aunt's stance.

They were about to entertain the gentlemen callers yet again. Aunt Penny did not wait for the girls to follow her but left once she had delivered her message.

Charlotte and Susan stood and checked their appearance. They chatted and giggled among themselves before continuing to the Music Room. Muriel followed them down the corridor, paused at the Breakfast Parlor, and then decided to move to the window for a look down the drive.

Coming up the drive, she saw Sir Nicholas in his high-perched phaeton accompanied, by the looks of it, by about a half dozen gentlemen, all on horseback. Behind that first party, a second, more substantial pack followed, just making the turn from the road. Their afternoon's guests would arrive very soon.

Instead of heading directly to the Music Room as Susan and Charlotte had, Muriel slipped down the corridor leading to the Grand Foyer to observe their company enter.

"Good afternoon to you, Mrs. Parker." Sir Nicholas

bowed from the waist. "I am only too happy to be of service once again."

Near the front door, several of the family's liveried footmen did whatever Huxley could not, collecting the numerous hats, walking sticks, and coats of the arriving gentlemen.

"Shall I direct the gentlemen to the Music Room?" Sir Nicholas suggested.

"Thank you. If you would, please lead the way." Aunt Penny nodded to the baronet to proceed.

Muriel thought she should move along before the men invaded the corridor where she now stood. With a sense of self-preservation, she continued down the corridor to the Music Room where Charlotte and Susan awaited. They quieted upon Muriel's entry, perhaps thinking she was one of the gentlemen.

"They are on their way now. I'm glad to see some of them have decided to return—there are even a few gentlemen I have never seen before." Muriel continued to the wall behind the pianoforte where the other instruments were displayed. She had left her flute on the side table after their practice.

"Why is it they all rushed off yesterday only to return today?" Susan wondered aloud.

"I believe there was something they wished to *discuss* in private," Muriel offered. She wasn't yet ready to include their dear friend in the sisters' ruse.

"Major Dunham!" Charlotte called out in welcome, alerting Susan and Muriel that they were no longer alone and should curtail their conversation regarding the guests. "Won't you please come in?"

Muriel noticed how beautiful Charlotte appeared standing next to the handsome major in his regimentals. The pink blush on her cheeks, the blue of her eyes, the green of her dress and matching grosgrain ribbon tied in a bow, draped from her golden curls piled high on the back of her head, made her the visual embodiment of spring.

The gentlemen continued to file in. Some stopped to speak with Susan, most moved directly to Charlotte, and all continued to behave themselves. No raised voices, heightened tempers, or pummeling fists.

Without a doubt, a good number of them were strategizing how to secure the front-row seats. If Muriel was not mistaken, Sir Nicholas, who stood off to one side with two other gentlemen, might be laying odds on that very prospect. If her father were at home, the baronet would have found himself escorted from the premises and none too gently, for he had been reprimanded for wagering on several occasions.

Muriel could not be certain what truly occupied him, but the hushed conversation and surreptitious glances made his conduct all the more suspect.

Within twenty minutes, the guests were seated, quiet, and awaiting the start of the first musical piece. Muriel took her position, with flute in hand, behind Susan, who sat at the pianoforte. Off to one side, money passed hands from a small group of gentlemen to Sir Nicholas.

Charlotte moved toward the harp, readying herself to

play. She tugged at the fingers of her glove, and the gentle-men silenced, sitting alert. There was an audible intake of breath when she drew off her left glove.

One might have thought they'd never seen a lady remove gloves before. A bare hand was not, in any way, risqué. Yet the men behaved as if she had raised the hem of her skirts, allowing them to view her ankle.

The performances were well received. Following the Mozart, Bach, and Vivaldi selections, Muriel and Susan moved aside. Charlotte sat at the pianoforte and began to play the final piece.

After a three-measure introduction, she sang. Her clear, heart-melting, sweet soprano rose above the audience, just out of their reach. All the gentlemen bore similar smitten expressions with their eyes widened, quite transfixed with the angelic quality of her voice. They sat tall in their chairs, chins tilted up to catch the ethereal notes.

When Muriel glanced beyond the last row, she saw *him* there, peering in from the rear of the room. Dressed in his traveling clothes, belcher scarf, brown jacket, buckskins, and hat in hand, he appeared much as a country gentle-men and not the usual dandified dress she'd expected.

Sir Philip had not been expected, but there he stood. He looked upon Charlotte with adoration. His usual dour smirk dissolved to the same serene, love-struck expression as those of the other gentlemen. The emotion must have caught him by surprise, for he staggered back from the door frame and disappeared, withdrawing from sight.

As much as his departure pleased her, Muriel was

afraid she had witnessed something remarkable—the very moment Sir Philip fell in love with Charlotte.

Philip pushed off the door frame and moved away from the Music Room. He could not yet force himself to pull his gaze from the sight of Lady Charlotte sitting at the keyboard of the pianoforte, no more than he could prevent himself from hearing the sweet notes. It was an image he'd not soon forget—if ever—nor the unexpected feeling that came forth from the sound of her voice.

He had come late, but not too late to experience the profound effect of her performance. It had captured the attention of the gentlemen who sat spellbound, captivated by Lady Charlotte's beauty and all her unexpected musical glory.

The stirring of emotion within Philip was one he had never felt before. He did not wished to acknowledge its existence because he feared what it meant.

It hadn't taken long. Less than a full measure? A few notes? Perhaps all it took was the rest between two notes. Those poor males trapped before her, in their seats, unable to move or escape from her presence.

Philip had learned only hours ago a new facet of this glorious diamond that made her now quite irresistible to him. She was not all mere musical talent and unparalleled beauty.

Farmer Gilbert had told Philip how he and his neighbors missed Lady Charlotte's visits. It had only been a few days since Bloxwich had been overrun by the London swells who had descended upon Faraday Hall.

The Duke's middle daughter had more than enough to occupy her time, yet she managed, in her absence, to arrange for delivery of her food baskets to those in need.

The young lady was truly in possession of a kind heart.

Philip had learned from Gilbert how, this last spring, she had come into his home when his wife Stella took ill with the fever. She'd immediately sent for Stella's sister, and while it took nearly a week, Lady Charlotte had seen to his children's care. At times she looked after the tykes herself. Apparently, this had not been the first or only time she had taken it upon herself to come to the aid of a tenant.

One would never guess she possessed such kindness that might only be rivaled by her social graces. Her qualities made her a woman he could truly love. On the other hand, there was no reason for her to look to Philip with fondness. It was clear that all these men seated before Charlotte vied for her interest.

Philip turned from the sight of her sitting at the pianoforte and realized his opinion of her had not mattered. Love should not be a contest, and with so many others competing for her favor, Philip had little hope that mutual affection between them would ever become evident.

After playing the final notes, Charlotte pulled her hands from the keyboard to a round of applause. The gentlemen were very kind. She felt a bit self-conscious singing before an audience, because she thought her voice sounded a bit thin and squeaky, but they seemed to enjoy it, or else they were prodigiously polite. But reassurances from Muriel, Susan, and Aunt Penny had convinced her she was in error. One could not judge one's own voice. She moved from the pianoforte and curtsied.

"*Brava,* Lady Charlotte!" several of the guests called out.

"*Encore!*" cried several more.

Charlotte smiled, pleased they had enjoyed her performance, and motioned for Susan and Muriel to join her at the head of the room. The three stood together with Charlotte in the center and bowed, concluding their performance.

"Thank you, gentlemen," Aunt Penny interrupted, and the room fell into a hush. "If you all will be so good as to remove to the east lawn, we will be serving tea."

There was a scuffle as the young men from the front row jostled for the chance to escort Charlotte.

"Sir Edwin, Major Dunham . . . there will be no violence," Charlotte reminded them. Her soft-spoken words quieted any disturbance.

Both gentlemen before her touched the bruises healing on their faces. This had not been their first altercation, she'd vow.

"Lord Henry, Mr. Emery, if you please." She met each of their gazes, confirming she had indeed chosen them for the honor of escorting her.

"Mr. Emery," Lord Henry acknowledged, inclining his head.

With equal respect, Mr. Emery returned the gesture. "Lord Henry," he returned.

The two gentlemen proudly offered Charlotte their arms for her escort.

Order and civility could be maintained, Charlotte reassured herself. The three of them led the company to the east lawn, where tables and chairs were clustered in threes and fours. The gentlemen would be seated, and it remained for the ladies to circulate among them, spending several minutes socializing with each group.

Susan approached Charlotte after nearly an hour had passed. "Char-Char, your hair ribbon is missing!"

Charlotte reached to the back of her head to discover that her ribbon was indeed absent. "Oh dear, that was one of my favorites!"

Lord Oscar leaped from his seat. "I shall find your ribbon for you, my lady."

"I shall be the one to retrieve your hair ornament, Lady Charlotte," Mr. Hughes replied.

"No, I shall be the one to find your ribbon!" Sir Wilfred shouted out.

"Why do you not offer a reward for the one who finds it? Just as you had for the victor of the footrace?" some clever gentleman shouted from the right.

It was a worthy suggestion, one Charlotte would not necessarily have thought of on her own. She glanced at her sister.

With an impish smile and a nod of her head, Muriel urged her to consent.

"Very well, gentlemen, if that is what you all truly wish." Charlotte glanced around, regarding them. This was not at all what she had planned for the afternoon.

They shouted their approval. The gentlemen had taken to their feet, excited to begin the new quest.

"I would like it returned, in any case." Charlotte would need to think up some suitable reward. "Whoever finds my green ribbon will be rewarded with—" She paused, considering what should be chosen for the prize. "I shall reveal a second secret, something of a personal nature, to the gentleman who returns my wayward ribbon."

The men cheered and disbursed, running from her in all directions. Charlotte thought they might have feared a second revelation, a second horrifying bit about her, a second blemish to accompany her wayward eye.

What type of imperfection would she possess? If Charlotte could not invent a believable blemish soon, she would need to consult Muriel, who would certainly have a suitable answer.

Chapter Nine

Y ou mean to tell me the gentlemen have decided upon a quest of their own? How did that happen? Did you somehow manage to maneuver them into . . . ?" Muriel couldn't imagine her sister manipulating anyone, but to believe her suitors actually asked for a second contest seemed ridiculous.

"It was not I, Moo. For the life of me I cannot think they'd wish to hear something as horrid as the nonsense about my eye," Charlotte told her. "They insisted. I did not have the heart to deny them—and I confess I desire the return of my lost hair ribbon."

"I suppose it will all work out. Perhaps not to their benefit, and it cannot harm yours." Muriel had no part in this bit of mischief, which some might not believe, but in this instance she could claim innocence. "What are you going to tell them?"

"I haven't yet considered . . ." Charlotte was clearly distracted by something. Here she stood, but her thoughts appeared to be very far away.

"Char-Char!" Muriel had never seen her sister behave in such an odd fashion. "You do not attend!"

"I do beg your pardon, Moo. What is it you were saying?" Charlotte blinked as if she had awoken from a sleep. It was most peculiar how she appeared to be participating in conversation one moment and then drifting off in the next, right before Muriel's eyes.

"Those gentlemen, the ones searching for your hair ribbon, are expecting you to—" Muriel noticed her sister's concentration waning. "Where are your thoughts?"

"Please forgive me." Charlotte let out a sigh. "I'm afraid I cannot keep my mind from drifting to *him*."

Muriel was very afraid she referred to that odious man.

"I did not see him this afternoon. I do not believe he attended." Charlotte glanced down at the toe of her slipper emerging from under the hem of her dress. She turned the pointed tip as if admiring the ornamentation. "How I wished he had seen me play, listened to me sing. I had hoped he might enjoy . . ."

Unquestionably she referred to that man who had foisted his presence upon them at Faraday Hall. He was an unwanted guest; Muriel did not even wish to think his name. "You cannot *like* him—Sir Philip."

"He thinks no more of me than one of his discarded neckcloths." Charlotte's voice broke at the very lowering thought. Revealing her despondent mood, she uttered a dramatic, "I am cast aside."

"If that were the case, then I would surely dub me an uncooperative length of linen," Muriel replied. Her revulsion to him was only second to his obvious distaste for her. "But all those other men adore you. Surely there must be one among them who would capture your heart."

"It would not be necessary if only Sir Philip . . ." Charlotte did not finish her thought.

"Why do you concern yourself about him?" Muriel hoped she'd been wrong about Sir Philip falling in love with Charlotte during her solo performance. She could not understand why Charlotte continually thought of the baronet. Redirecting her attention to a lucky gentleman, one who would prove to be more deserving, is what she needed to do.

"What of the young man who returns your ribbon?" Muriel prodded, as if she had asked the question a dozen times. With the ribbon's discovery, Charlotte would divulge to the victor her favorite dress or pair of shoes or whatever it was she'd deem a proper reward.

"I beg your pardon, Moo?" Charlotte's thoughts were miles away.

"What will you say to the one who returns your hair ribbon? You must have something prepared," Muriel whispered. "Have you planned some unfortunate, undesirable trait to tell him?"

"That doesn't sound much like a reward to me, Moo." At this moment Charlotte did not seem very concerned with her situation. It might be only a manner of minutes before the discovery of her ribbon.

"You're just blue-deviled because of Sir Philip, and he is not worth the effort. Do not forget the reason all these gentlemen are present." Muriel began to think she would never be able to rid her sister of the plaguing thoughts of the baronet.

"Do not worry, Moo," Charlotte sniffed. "I shall think of something eventually. And I shan't fret over *him;* there is no need. What do I care if he does not think well of me?"

"Char-Char." Muriel laid a hand upon her arm to stress the importance of her words. "Do you not think that being the center of attention for nearly two dozen men is enough? Most ladies would be thrilled."

"Of course it is thrilling." But the truth was, Charlotte did not think as much of them as she did of Sir Philip.

It was of no consequence. Charlotte would not dare go where she was not wanted—and that place was near Sir Philip's heart. As Muriel had stated, she had nearly two dozen eager suitors to pay her court. It was about time she considered them and addressed their interest in her.

"Mr. Evans, you have returned!" Aunt Penny called out, glancing toward Charlotte, making sure she was alerted to her victor's arrival.

Handsome, wavy-haired Mr. Evans appeared, dressed in a double-breasted cutaway coat, buff kerseymere trousers, and top boots. He held the green ribbon high in the air, displaying his triumph.

Muriel took her sister by the hand and moved toward him. "Bravo, Mr. Evans. Wherever did you find it?"

"Apparently as the guests moved from the Music Room to where we took refreshment, this ribbon decided it wished to remain indoors." He laid it over the Clarence-blue forearm of his jacket and offered it to Charlotte. "It lay on the floor behind a leg of the pianoforte."

"Thank you so very much." Charlotte blinked up at him, accepting her beloved ribbon. "I wonder how it could possibly have managed to be there."

"No matter, Mr. Evans has found it. You must *tell him*, Charlotte. He must have his reward," Muriel urged her sister. "You have promised."

Charlotte found a suitable place to sit and handed her ribbon to Muriel. "Will you replace it, dearest?"

Muriel fastened the ribbon in Charlotte's hair and tied it more securely than Lydia had.

Mr. Evans looked on. He preened, fingering his shirt frill and stock, waiting patiently.

"You shall have your prize." Charlotte smiled at him, which might have felt to him reward enough. She stood when Muriel had finished and stepped away. Charlotte held out her hand and beckoned, "Your arm, sir."

"I would be most delighted, my lady."

Once Charlotte placed her hand upon Mr. Evans' arm, they strolled toward the parterre. Charlotte gently guided him in the correct direction with a wave of her hand.

Muriel had no idea what Charlotte planned to tell him.

"I must see to the other gentlemen," Aunt Penny informed her niece.

As her aunt walked away, Muriel caught sight of someone new approaching. Dressed in a dark green jacket and smooth buff-colored trousers, Sir Philip neared.

"I see your sister has found her champion," he commented, sounding almost as if he did not care.

"Yes, there is some interest there." The best Muriel could do was make the baronet believe Charlotte had designs upon Mr. Evans.

"I had not thought myself interested, in regards to— However, now I must admit . . ." Sir Philip sounded almost unhappy at his realization. "I find I am having second thoughts about your sister."

She knew it. Muriel knew the dratted Sir Philip had fallen in love with Charlotte, when he'd all but convinced himself that Charlotte could not possibly come close to the suitable wife he had imagined. How could he have changed his mind so quickly?

Sir Philip's gaze moved to the few gentlemen who milled about, readying to depart. Perhaps he was sizing up his competition. If a choice of a husband were up to Muriel, it would have been simple enough. She would approve of anyone *except* Sir Philip.

Arriving at the stone bench in the parterre, Mr. Evans took up Charlotte's hand, holding it near, and gazed upon her with wide eyes.

"My dear Lady Charlotte, I am so very fortunate to have this opportunity to be in your company. I know I met you only a few days ago, but I must confess I find myself quite besotted. And I must tell you, I am not to be dissuaded."

"What was that again?" Charlotte said, turning to face him.

She had walked alongside him the entire way here but did not remember much of the journey. She barely recalled leaving Muriel's company or turning the corner of the manor. Had she and Mr. Evans conversed as they strolled? Charlotte couldn't imagine what she might have said to him.

Her attention had drifted upon seeing what she thought was a solitary horseman arriving just moments ago, coming up the drive. She had thought it might have been, possibly could be, Sir Philip.

"I'm afraid I didn't hear you." Then the notion of what she should say came to her.

Mr. Evans wished to hear of some deficit she hid from the masses. Tell him, she would—but it would be a lie, and lying did not sit well with her. Even a little one. Oh, why did they insist she do this to them?

"I'm afraid I don't hear well on my left side." She brought her hand to her left ear, indicating her difficulty.

"You can't hear, you say?" Mr. Evans' devotion seemed to be wavering a bit.

Charlotte thought Mr. Evans needed some added incentive to question his affection for her. "Not to be dissuaded," he had told her.

"Excuse me? Might you repeat that? And please stand over here." She gestured to her right. "My partial hearing does not bother you, does it?" Charlotte felt that if he truly cared for her, it should not make the least bit of difference.

"It cannot matter to me." Mr. Evans did not sound

entirely convinced, however. How did he expect Charlotte to believe him?

"That is good to know. I imagine you have already heard about my eye?"

"Oh, that . . ." His voice faltered and he staggered back a few steps.

"You must come closer to speak"—Charlotte reached out to draw him near—"else I cannot properly hear you."

"I had thought that was a load of gammon," he said, raising his voice, nearly shouting at her. "A bit of unpleasantness to put some of us off."

"I cannot tell you how pleased I am those things do not bother you. Now we may be truly comfortable with each other."

"Yes." He pasted on a smile that even Charlotte knew to be false.

"I also wish to tell you that my favorite flowers are tulips." She smiled, waiting to see how he would react to that.

"Tulips," he repeated flatly. It did not seem to please him.

"Yes, they bloom in the spring when the cold of winter fades and the days grow warmer." Charlotte continued to watch him. Then to gently remind him, she offered, "If I am not mistaken, you brought me several tied with a white satin ribbon the day after we met."

"Did I?" But his heart really wasn't in his reply, nor was there any ardor. The devotion that he had proclaimed for her only minutes earlier had evaporated. "Oh, yes. I believe you are correct."

"As if you could have forgotten." She smiled and fluttered her lashes.

He consulted his pocket watch. "I beg your pardon, but I do believe it is time I be on my way. Again I thank you for this opportunity, Lady Charlotte." He bowed over her hand and then headed for the stables. "I shall never forget this moment."

It seemed that Mr. Evans could not leave fast enough.

No matter. Just as Muriel had told her, it was a test of his affection. It seemed Mr. Evans had discarded any interest he may have had.

Her sister's plan had not just come close but gone beyond what Charlotte considered correct behavior. She could not deny she was leading these gentlemen to believe what she would like to think of as *exaggerated* truths.

She followed his path out of the parterre toward the stables and stopped at the edge of the house. The sight of Mr. Evans departing on his horse did not mean as much as the vision of a crested carriage coming up the long drive of Faraday Hall.

Pure hope and happiness filled Charlotte's heart. "Look!" she cried out to no one. "Papa returns!"

Chapter Ten

Charlotte rounded the corner and headed toward the terrace where she'd left Susan, Muriel, and her aunt.

"Where have the other gentlemen gone, Moo?" Charlotte glanced about. She could see no trace of anyone near the maze or the east lawn where they'd gathered for tea earlier.

"They left moments after Mr. Evans returned with your ribbon," Aunt Penny told her.

"I see." Charlotte had wished to tell Muriel, and only Muriel, what had transpired during her private audience with Mr. Evans. "I saw Papa's carriage pull off the road and come up the drive."

"Your father has returned? We must hurry to greet him." Aunt Penny wasted no time and rushed toward the house.

Charlotte made to follow, but Muriel stopped her by taking hold of her elbow.

"Char-Char, what did you say to Mr. Evans?"

"I told him my favorite flowers were tulips."

"There was something else, perhaps?" Muriel pressed her to continue.

"I had mentioned some difficulty hearing on my left side." Charlotte motioned to her ear and straightened her shoulders, still uncomfortable with the outright lie. "He took it to mean I was deaf."

"That was well done." Muriel chuckled. "Very clever."

"It doesn't feel clever at all. It is entirely untrue. And I think it's almost cruel, Moo. The moment we were alone he told me he did not care about the prize. He wished only to share my company, if just for a few minutes."

"And I vow it took only a few seconds for Mr. Evans to change his opinion of you." By the sound of Muriel's voice, she was disappointed in him as well.

"Yes, I suppose that's exactly what happened. He does not truly care for me." Charlotte's gaze dropped to her feet, feeling close to tears.

"I am sorry," said Muriel, but she did not sound sincere. "You could not have cared for Mr. Evans all that much; you've only just made his acquaintance."

"It is not *him* precisely," Charlotte confessed. "I am disappointed by how easily the gentlemen are appalled by the slightest blemish and then exaggerate them."

"I believe it best that we not mention this to Papa," said Muriel as she glanced at the house, looking to make sure they had not been overheard. "He might not look so kindly upon this should he learn of it."

"I agree." Charlotte never enjoyed keeping anything from him.

"Shall we see Papa now?" Muriel suggested.

"Yes, let us go at once." Charlotte braved a smile, grasped her younger sister's arm, and moved toward the house.

Muriel and Charlotte entered in time to meet their father and Aunt Penny in the Grand Foyer.

"Yes, I completely understand. Thank you for handling the matter with such delicacy, Mrs. Parker," the Duke said.

Charlotte and Muriel stopped upon seeing their father and chorused, "Papa!" They curtsied and then ran toward him, arms open wide to hug him tight.

"We have missed you so!" his daughters cried. "We are glad you are home."

"The two of you have had quite the adventure." Their father returned their affection with a welcoming smile. "And my lovely Charlotte—it seems the young men could not wait for you to come to Town. They came to you."

"I am sorry, Papa. I had not meant to cause problems."

"I do not blame you. You have managed the best you could." The Duke stepped back and motioned behind them. "See who I have brought with me."

So excited was Muriel, and apparently Charlotte, to see their father, they had not noticed Sir Samuel Pruitt, now standing with Aunt Penny.

"Sir Samuel!" Charlotte and Muriel called out. They curtsied and each offered him their hand in greeting. He looked to be in good health. His wide, dark eyes and generous smile displayed his excitement at his arrival.

"Lady Charlotte." Sir Samuel took her hand first. "Lady Muriel." He bowed over her hand next. "I am delighted to see the two of you again."

"We saw you just last autumn, did we not?" Charlotte ventured, glancing at her sister for corroboration.

"Yes, before our first snowfall, as I recall," Muriel added. He had been on his way to his family home, Hamsdale Heath, in Northumberland.

"You must tell us how your sister and brothers are getting on," Charlotte urged.

"And you must tell me news of Augusta and her husband. I have not had a letter from her in some time," Sir Samuel insisted.

Aunt Penny interrupted, "I am sure that all your conversations can wait until after Sir Samuel has settled in his room and recuperated from his journey."

"As you request, Mrs. Parker," Sir Samuel acknowledged. "I shall see you both at supper and we will speak then."

"But Sir Samuel—" Muriel thought his premature departure was grossly unfair.

"Papa—" Charlotte pleaded, hoping their father might intervene on their behalf.

"You shall see him at supper," he said in a tone that would brook no protest. "We've spent many hours on the roads. You must allow our guest to properly rest. Now off with you, Sir Samuel. There will be plenty of opportunity for discussion and family gossip later."

"Very well." Muriel did so wish to have a long conversation with him, and not just about their families. "I suppose I shall need to wait."

"That's my girl." The Duke smiled and gestured for them to follow. "If you please, ladies. I would like to speak to the two of you."

Charlotte took hold of Muriel's hand and they followed their father to his library. The room felt complete when he entered. The walls of leather-bound books seemed to welcome the Duke.

"I am quite fond of that young man." His Grace had meant Sir Samuel, of course.

"As are we," Charlotte answered for the two of them.

"If either of you could see about matrimonially securing him, I'd be more than grateful." The Duke winked at his daughters.

"Oh, Papa, you shouldn't tease us so." Charlotte pulled the door closed behind them.

"Char-Char does have a dozen or so suitors presently doting on her; one more shouldn't make a difference." Muriel squeezed her sister's arm, letting her know her words were spoken as a mere jest. "I'll see what I can do Papa, although I am only fifteen."

"Soon to be sixteen, although I do not believe I could part with you so soon." He walked behind his desk, glanced at the papers that had accumulated on its surface since his absence, and settled into the chair. "Now tell me what has transpired since these suitors of Charlotte's arrived. Your aunt seems to be most distressed by their presence."

"Every one of them is worthy and wonderful." Charlotte could only manage to say good things about their gentlemen visitors . . . or about anyone, truth be told.

"I would expect to hear nothing less from you, my dear Charlotte." The Duke turned to his youngest. "What say you, Muriel?"

Muriel glanced at her sister before giving an opinion. "There has never been such a gathering of suitors. Not since Augusta's party, but you must multiply their number by three."

"After receiving Mrs. Parker's missive I did notice the lack of young men in Town. I believe she was correct deciding you should remain in the country." The Duke shrugged and exhaled. "What is the use of going to Town if half its inhabitants are here? Just before I left, I heard many more were planning to vacate, to the dismay of the Almack's Patronesses."

"Lord and Lady Hopkins plan a ball for their daughter Lady Margaret tomorrow night," Charlotte informed him.

"I've heard they have invited many families to stay with them, simply switching the venue from their townhouse in London to their country house." The Duke glanced thoughtfully at his daughters. "Shall we open Faraday Hall and invite house guests as well?"

Muriel wished Aunt Penny were present to help make the decisions. "We do not have as many distractions here in Essex as they have in Town," she said. "I think we have more than enough to do, planning entertainment every afternoon for this last week and who knows for how much longer."

"Not only is Sir Samuel here, but we also have Sir Philip staying with us," Charlotte quickly added. "He resides in the Gold Suite until his curricle is repaired."

"Who is this Sir Philip?" The Duke looked up from his desk.

Charlotte brightened and answered, "Sir Philip Somerville met with some misfortune a few days ago while traveling the roads not far from here. With so many other visitors making Bloxwich their residence, the poor man had no choice but to invite himself to remain with us. I shall introduce you at supper."

"I see." Their father's interest waned and he rubbed his eyes. He also looked fatigued after the day's travel. "I cannot say if I will dine with you tonight."

"Then you shall make his acquaintance in the morning," Charlotte promised.

"Yes," Muriel agreed, trying to keep her distaste for their guest to herself. "His presence seems quite unavoidable."

Everyone gathered in the Blue Parlor after the dinner gong had sounded. The Duke, as he had predicted, was noticeably absent.

"I had looked forward to meeting His Grace." Sir Philip stood near the center of the room and spoke to no one in particular.

Muriel noticed his black dinner jacket and cream-colored knee breeches. Was it possible they came from that very small leather trunk of his? How many items of clothing could that thing hold?

"Just as he wished to make your acquaintance, I'm sure," Charlotte returned, blinking wide-eyed at the baronet.

"Will you do me the honor of allowing me to escort you into the Dining Room, Lady Charlotte?" Sir Samuel pivoted from Muriel to Charlotte and stepped toward her.

"I had wished to have that honor," the taller, fair-haired Sir Philip remarked.

"Is that so?" Sir Samuel replied, but not in any threatening manner.

"I'm sure we can settle this matter like civilized gentlemen," Sir Philip said, moving toward Charlotte.

"You're not speaking of crossing swords, are you?" Sir Samuel glanced at the ladies. "Before partaking our evening meal?"

"Of course not. I abhor violence." Sir Philip stood his ground, but did not bully the young Sir Samuel.

Muriel could not deny he was a man after her sister's own heart. Charlotte blinked up at Sir Philip. Was Charlotte thinking he was the most perfect man for her? Muriel wondered.

"Ah, perhaps we should see who has the most intricately tied cravat?" Sir Samuel suggested.

"Nonsense," Sir Philip said, stepping back and sweeping his hand toward Charlotte. "We shall allow the lady to decide between us."

Charlotte blushed. Her smile widened for Sir Samuel, knowing full well, as Muriel had, he would be all that was understanding and allow her to choose Sir Philip over him for her escort.

"Sir Philip." Charlotte held out her hand, waiting for him to respond.

"I am greatly honored." Sir Philip bowed at the waist before offering his arm.

"I suppose you are left with me to lead you in to dinner," Sir Samuel said to Muriel, and glanced about. "What of Mrs. Parker, will she not be joining us at the table?"

Muriel could not be happier to be left in the care of Sir Samuel. "My aunt should arrive shortly. I cannot imagine what is keeping her."

Aunt Penny entered the Blue Parlor only moments later and Sir Samuel escorted both ladies into the Dining Room.

Following their meal, the women prepared to leave the two men to their port. Aunt Penny instructed the girls to remove to the Citrus Parlor, while she excused herself, saying she needed to speak to the Duke. Sir Philip and Sir Samuel claimed they had no wish to remain without the ladies. In truth, Muriel suspected, the gentlemen probably did not wish to be alone with each other.

Sir Samuel offered Muriel his arm to escort her to the Citrus Parlor, and Sir Philip, escorting Charlotte, followed directly.

As much as Muriel loathed to leave Charlotte to Sir Philip's attention, her conversation with Sir Samuel could not be delayed any longer. She led him to the far side of the room so as not to be disturbed.

Charlotte settled at one end of the green-leaf-patterned sofa just inside the room. She removed her gloves and retrieved her embroidery hoop from the basket. To her delight, Sir Philip joined her, occupying the other end of the sofa. She attempted to keep her focus upon the needlework before her and soon detected Sir Philip studying the stitches. Charlotte turned her hoop, allowing him an unobstructed view.

"Somehow I thought your work depicted some sort of animal." A most quizzical expression crossed his face. "A dog, perhaps?"

Did the simple wildflowers not please him? Had he wished she had chosen to portray a hunt or a woodland scene with wildlife?

"No, I— Oh!" Charlotte knew exactly to what he referred. "Muriel is working on a depiction of Romulus and Remus with the nurturing Lupa—she's a wolf. Perhaps that is what you saw?"

"I suppose that might have been," he replied.

Charlotte glanced at the basket that held their evening occupation. She could not imagine how he should come to have seen her sister's hoop instead of her own.

He gazed upon her work again, only now he seemed more pleased at what he saw. Charlotte read the admiration in his eyes, the first sign of affection for her, perhaps. She hoped.

"No, matter," said Sir Philip, handing back her hoop and taking her hand in his, hesitant to release his hold. The feel of his gloved hand on her bare skin made her feel quite light-headed.

"I feel your pulse racing," he said.

It was. A flush of warmth crept up her neck to her

cheeks when she realized something had altered between them. Indeed, there was a complete difference in the way Sir Philip addressed her this evening.

Perhaps it was her imagination. Had she dreamed he pressed her hand as well? And the spark of interest she thought she had detected in his eyes? Charlotte thought not.

If her last breath were to be exhaled at that moment, she would have no complaints. If she were to expire on this very spot, Charlotte was certain she would head straight for heaven.

Chapter Eleven

Charlotte had sat before her dressing table the next evening and endured the hair tongs and styling for nearly two hours. Now she stood in the center of her room and waited for Lydia to return.

The abigail helped Charlotte dress, tying the many tapes to secure her gown in place.

"I cannot tell you how fortunate it is that everyone has taken the afternoon to prepare for the Hopkins' ball tonight," Charlotte said, remaining still while Lydia moved from one side to the other. "I do not think I could have managed to entertain callers *and* attend the dance this evening."

"I imagine everyone is anxious for tonight's festivities," said Lydia, as she tucked the excess length of the tapes into the gown, shielding them from view.

"Do you expect he'll think me pretty tonight?" Charlotte peered over her shoulder at the full-length mirror. An unfinished work of art, she regarded herself in the glass, imagining her overall impression in the near-white gown.

A soft, sky blue color would have been more flattering. However, all her new gowns were some variation of white, for that was what young ladies attending their first Season wore, and that is what had been ordered with the exception of only a few other colors.

Lydia smiled, wide-eyed, admiring the young mistress. "I cannot imagine a gentleman who would not notice you, Lady Charlotte. I 'spect you know that already."

"I would never make such a presumption. I don't expect anyone would find me *that* attractive."

Charlotte had been reminded of her beauty all her life. Truth be told, she found this talk about her outward appearance very superficial. Everyone knew her to possess great beauty, and she would do what she could to fulfill their expectations. But, she wondered, what of her hopes for this evening?

Would she manage to dance with every man she wished? Then Charlotte thought of Sir Philip—the only man she truly wished to share a dance with. Even though he did not stand with her suitors, and had not made demands upon her time, could she, in good conscience, consider reserving a dance for him? He might not even ask her tonight. Oh, that was a sad thought.

"Who is it you wish to take particular notice?" Muriel announced her presence with her question, peering around the bedchamber door. "Aunt Penny is asking for you, Lydia. I'll finish pinning Char-Char's dress."

"Thank you, m'lady." After an uneasy glance, the abigail quit the room.

Muriel, who had finished her toilette, collected some straight pins and moved to her sister's side to complete the work Lydia had started. "I had not thought you preferred any one of your suitors over another."

Charlotte had the distinct impression Muriel would not approve of the gentleman she held in particular regard and was hesitant to name him.

When Muriel tugged at the bodice edges, pulling them closer, Charlotte cried out, "Take care, will you, Moo?"

"You wouldn't be thinking of a man such as Sir Philip, perhaps?" Muriel's accusing stare was leveled over Charlotte's shoulder in the mirror.

"A man such as Sir Philip?" Charlotte wished to know exactly what her sister had meant.

"Do you think that sort of man cares a whit about the appearance of anyone except himself?" Muriel's gaze moved down to her hands, busy pinning the edge of Charlotte's garment. "Honestly, Char-Char, I'm quite convinced his only concern is the cut of his coat and the fit of his trousers."

Charlotte could not fault him for his attention to his appearance. It must take quite a bit of effort to maintain his image. He traveled without a valet and with limited apparel, no more than could fit in a bandbox.

"I imagine if he truly cared for me," she uttered, "I would be cherished above his starched creations."

"Char-Char, you are hopeless!"

"Why do you have such a low opinion of him?" A second yank to her midsection made Charlotte cry out.

"Moo! Why are you pulling so tight? Are you certain you know what you are doing?"

Muriel glanced at her sister's reflection with a mischievous glimmer in her eye. "Never fear, Char-Char, I know exactly what I'm doing."

"One might think you were purposely causing me discomfort!" Charlotte tried to catch her breath.

"Of course not," Muriel denied, as if it were the most absurd accusation. "That you should compare yourself to an item of clothing is ridiculous. What makes you sure he is a man who could care for you—for yourself— just as your other suitors?"

Charlotte did her best to remain as still as possible. She did not wish to encourage her sister to mistakenly place a straight pin into her side. "He makes every effort to look his best. There is nothing wrong with that. Is that not what I am doing this very minute?"

"And with good reason. You have a great many men dangling after you," Muriel reminded her. "I should think they would take precedence over our unexpected house-guest, who only came upon us by pure chance."

Muriel did have a point. Beyond Charlotte's idyllic musings that he might be interested in her, he had not clearly shown any sign of forming an attachment.

"That should be adequate." Muriel admired her work and stepped back from Charlotte. "I would be quite shocked to learn that he actually cares for anyone other than himself. I do not believe he has shown the least interest in becoming one of your suitors."

That much was true. None of Charlotte's hopeful

thoughts or overly optimistic wishes could change Sir Philip's intentions toward her. She would just have to admit he did not think of her as anything other than the daughter of his host.

Muriel sat anxiously in the carriage during the half-hour drive to The Acorns. Once they arrived, Charlotte might find it difficult or nearly impossible to remove herself from the squabs. It wasn't the number of straight pins Muriel used to fasten her sister's dress but the direction in which she lined the pins, or rather, the sharp ends.

Muriel had placed the needle-sharp ends facing outward in various seams. She did this to protect her sister from any dancing partner who moved too close to her or who came into contact with any of those restricted areas.

The Duke of Faraday stepped into the foyer followed by his two daughters and their aunt. The Duke had relinquished his hat, cape, and cane. He now stood with some other gentlemen acquaintances while waiting for the remainder of his party.

Muriel unfastened the clasp at the neck of Charlotte's mantle, while Charlotte's cloak seemed to have snagged upon the shoulder of her gown.

"I think one of my pins must have caught on the lining." Charlotte turned to inspect her garment.

Muriel moved very quickly, tossing off her outerwear, and rushed to her sister's side. "Allow me to check." She moved Charlotte's hands aside and made a thorough inspection. "Never fear, everything is as it should be."

"Let us move along, girls," Aunt Penny urged her nieces, guiding them from the foyer toward the ballroom. They waited at the door until they were announced.

Muriel admired her sister under the light of the sparkling crystal chandeliers. The soft white silk of her dress with the slight hint of pink accentuated the attractive blush upon her cheeks and brought out the clear, bright blue of her wide eyes.

"I do beg your pardon, Aunt Penny." Muriel had backed into her aunt while stepping out of the way of a half dozen young bucks who dashed toward her sister. "I wonder which lucky man will partner Char-Char for the first dance?"

"I believe it should prove very interesting," said Aunt Penny, paying rapt attention to the interactions around her.

Across the room, Muriel spied Sir Philip in conversation with several men. A few of them were Charlotte's suitors, but apparently not as ardent as the ones who had just nearly trampled her in their pursuit of her sister.

Although Muriel did not stand among them, she was privy to their conversation. She watched them carefully as they spoke, observing their every word, or nearly so.

"I am not convinced these tales are true," Sir Philip told them, tapping his quizzing glass on his cheek.

"I cannot verify the tale to be true, but I have heard it said she suffers from weak eyes," Lord Oscar told them.

"Weak? She cannot see beyond her fingertips!" a gentleman sporting a violet waistcoat nearly matching the color of his blackened eye announced.

"I have heard it is only one of many afflictions," Sir Hugh Linville corrected. "I do not find it disturbing in the least. Hardly noticeable, I say."

"Hardly noticeable?" Local gentry Mr. Lawrence balked at the baronet's words. "The eye is glass, pure and simple. If you were to gaze into them both, one could clearly see the difference. The right eye, although a most beautiful but not at all realistic color, does not by half match the true blue hue of her left!"

"Most gents seem to agree completely!" The speaker gestured to those gentlemen standing across the room surrounding Charlotte, trying to secure a dance.

"It don't matter," said Sir Hugh. "The girl's simply a vision. What does it matter if she—" He now had his back to Muriel, causing her to miss what he said next.

"What about her hearing?" the man with the violet waistcoat put forward for discussion.

"Hearing? She's hardly deaf, my man." Sir Hugh came to Charlotte's defense yet again. "She merely has difficulty with her hearing in her left ear."

"If any one of these other lovely young ladies happened to suffer the same ailment, I warrant they'd rather breathe their last than make that confession, don't you know."

Sir Philip did not appear shocked at the news, keeping his facade impassive. At least word of Charlotte's infirmities had finally made their way to him.

"Lady Muriel." Sir Samuel, who stood before her, having called her name once, spoke louder. "You are quite beautiful this evening. I daresay when it is time for your come-out, you shall cause as much of a stir as your sisters."

"There is no need to waste such a heartfelt compliment on me, Sir Samuel," Muriel scolded him, albeit playfully.

"Acknowledging beauty is never wasted." A bow of his head conveyed his sincerity. "Would you honor me with the first dance?"

"It is nothing personal, my dear friend. I confess there must be some young lady who would actually enjoy dancing, especially with you."

Their hostess, Lady Hopkins, followed by two young ladies, approached. The three of them eyed Sir Samuel with more than casual interest. Muriel took a half-step forward, shielding him from their prying gazes.

"Allow me to make known to you my daughter Margaret's very good friends from Town," Lady Hopkins began.

That was when Muriel and Sir Samuel became acquainted with Lady Julia Monroe and Miss Sophie Prichard. Sir Samuel's further misfortune led to his first dance with Miss Prichard. Lady Hopkins went on her way, leaving Muriel to stand with Lady Julia.

"The lovely Lady Charlotte is your sister?" Lady Julia's gaze moved from Muriel to Charlotte, who now stood up with Lord Henry. "I believe I can understand why the whole of London has relocated to this village. She is very lovely and so very graceful."

The attention of all who overheard their conversation focused upon the dance floor where, to Muriel's embarrassment, Charlotte promptly stumbled.

Lady Julia gasped, crying out.

Muriel merely gazed toward the heavens. In the future, her sister would be known as the very lovely and *not* so graceful Charlotte.

"I wonder if you might oblige me, m'dear." The pompous intonation of the familiar, of the superfluous, of the one and only Sir Philip addressed her. He held up his hand, staying Muriel's unwanted reply. "I have already had the extreme pleasure of making Lady Julia's acquaintance. I thank you."

So there was no puffing him off on her. Lady Julia stood there wide-eyed and seemingly more than willing to accept the baronet's attentions, only to be disappointed.

"I feel I must honor my host by extending the courtesy of dancing with his daughter." Sir Philip glanced around, clearly looking for Charlotte.

Had he no notion that all Charlotte's dances were taken? If by chance Charlotte learned of Sir Philip's desire to partner her, she might do the unthinkable and arrange to accommodate his request.

Muriel would make the ultimate sacrifice for her sister

by dancing, an exercise that she admittedly loathed, with Sir Philip, whom she loathed more.

"Thank you, sir. I should be delighted." Muriel was far from any thought of satisfaction when it came to sharing company with Sir Philip.

"You?" he cried, undoubtedly not pleased, but he could not have been more unhappy than Muriel herself. "Very well. Shall we take this opportunity to make our way closer to the dance floor?"

She placed her gloved hand upon his and they stepped toward the center of the room. How Muriel dreaded his company. It was for the greater good, she told herself. Repeatedly.

Sir Philip chuckled, surely not with delight.

"What is it?" It surprised Muriel to see his normally unpleasant, stoic visage transformed into a pleasant, almost agreeable expression.

"If there were a contest to see who had the tallest shirt points, I daresay Lord Wells and Sir Evelyn Harrison would win." Sir Philip pointed out two gentlemen standing on the other side of the room. "If one should lean close and whisper to the other, I think someone's eye would be put out."

Men's apparel humor. It was not in the least amusing to Muriel.

"Look there, I believe Lord Stanton has designs upon your sister." Sir Philip might have thought his voice held a trace of apathy, but Muriel detected a protective quality in his tone.

Lord Stanton hovered near the dancers, obviously

eager to partner Charlotte for the next set. Lord Henry's stern glances to the awaiting Lord Stanton warned him not to approach. His posture stiffened perceptively, and it appeared he was no longer enjoying himself on the dance floor.

Noting the silent drama, Sir Philip remarked, "You should not wish me to remain here idle. You cannot intervene, but I may upon your request." He tensed, ready to leap to Charlotte's aid.

"You'll do no such thing." Muriel thought it shocking he should act as her sister's champion.

Lord Henry extended his arm behind Charlotte, unwilling to relinquish his limited possession of her during his promised dance. "Odd's fish!" he cried, pulling away from her as if bitten, and rubbed his forearm.

Charlotte leaped from him at his oath.

Muriel hid behind her open fan, partially out of a small measure of guilt and partially so no one could see her laugh.

"What goes on there?" Sir Philip raised his quizzing glass to observe the commotion.

The straight pins Muriel had placed in her sister's bodice had succeeded in keeping the gentlemen at a proper distance, and the ball was just getting started.

Charlotte wondered if *he* had been looking at her. She could have hoped for as much, but doubted it. Sir Philip stood with Muriel, and it appeared as if they were waiting to take their places for the next dance.

Why had he asked Muriel? Even more impossible to understand was why her sister had accepted.

Charlotte would have loved to stand across from him, pass close to him during the steps of the dance, near enough to smell his cologne and feel the warmth of his hand against hers. But it was not to be.

"Lady Charlotte?" Lord Stanton nearly shouted at her, for he had called to her several times and she had rudely not even noticed.

"I am sorry, my lord." Charlotte had been caught staring at another man. She would hate to admit such an indiscretion to one of her most attentive suitors. "You inquire about your dance?" With a gift of a smile she extended her gloved hand. "Yes, it is indeed time."

Charlotte took his arm and they stepped forward to take their place with the other couples. She stood across from him for the country dance. Glancing down the line, she spied Sir Philip, realizing he was only a few couples down.

He was, as always, immaculately dressed, from the crisp folds of his cravat against the black evening dress with silver waistcoat and white breeches to the clocked stockings and spotless black dancing slippers.

The music began. The dancers bowed to their partners. She stepped toward Lord Stanton and back into the ladies' line.

Charlotte turned away, taking the hand of the other gentleman in her foursome. Still she could not keep her attention from wandering to Sir Philip.

She caught her slipper, which nearly sent her to the floor. This had not been the first time this evening.

"I beg your pardon," she apologized. This was the second time she had taken a misstep. Normally she was not such a clumsy clod, but tonight . . . She had to admit she had eyes only for a certain baronet and not her current dancing partner, no matter who he might be.

For shame.

Again clasping her partner's hand, she moved to turn under their raised arms.

Had Lord Stanton not toiled, competed from the very first? He'd filled a pail full of gooseberries to earn him a place at tea with her. Then he'd raced across the green, in his stocking feet no less, to win the opportunity to learn something about her.

He hadn't won a challenge, yet he must have full knowledge of her wandering eye and difficulty hearing. He must truly love her, indeed.

Why had she found it so easy to look away from her own dancing partner? Devoted, attentive Lord Stanton. And here Charlotte pined for another man.

Lord Stanton was well connected and handsome, and would come into the title of earl just as Sir Philip would. But somehow the two men were not remotely the same.

Sir Philip did not have the obvious, traditional handsome visage. He was in possession of an attitude, a manner that bespoke total confidence. His face may have been perhaps a bit long, and his nose perhaps a bit big, and his mouth perhaps a bit wide.

During the dance, Sir Philip stepped lightly, with his

straight back and perfect arm positions. His toes were pointed and moved with graceful precision. Charlotte could not help but feel the sum of his parts created a man she could truly love and admire for a lifetime.

Chapter Twelve

For most of the Faraday Hall household, this was the morning following the Hopkins' ball. For Philip it was also the first day for his new valet.

"Good morning to you, Tom Sturgis," Philip greeted. "You look very fine this morning." He'd purchased suitable clothing for his new employee. Two days ago Philip insisted the young man bathe, have a fine meal, and get a good night's rest before meeting him at Faraday Hall for further instructions.

"And good day to you, Sir Philip." The boy stood taller, obviously proud of his appearance.

"Now what should we call you?" Philip figured he ought to have a new name to go along with his new position.

"Young Sturgis is usually what they calls me, on account o' my older brother Frank is Sturgis," he said. "You could call me Tom."

"What about Thomas?" Philip suggested.

"Aye, that'll do me fine." His smiled nearly reached from ear to ear.

"I see you've found my jacket and my boots." It pleased Philip that his directions were followed with aplomb.

"That I have, right where you said they'd be." Thomas raised his left arm, the one with his employer's draped jacket, and then lifted a pair of Hessians in the air.

"If you wish to remain in my service, I shall guarantee you a decent wage for equal effort. I shall retain your services for as long I am willing to employ you and you are willing to remain."

"I'll give it my best, gov."

"If you please, you should address me as *sir.*" Philip reminded himself this was Thomas' first day.

"'Scuse me, o' course. Yes, *sir.*"

"I expect to have need of your services for the entire stay in Town. When I am ready to depart for the country at the end of the summer, you shall have a letter of recommendation for subsequent employment. How does that sound?"

"Fair enough, sir," the young man replied. "I promise to do my best."

"Excellent." Philip nodded his head in agreement. "One other thing before you leave, Thomas."

"Yes, sir?"

"Even though I am your employer, I do still expect you to be your own man. Is that understood?" Philip did not care for a servant who scraped the floor, mindlessly following their employer's every direction.

"My own man— But, sir . . . I don't think I understand." Thomas adjusted his hold on the boots.

Philip brought a fist to his pursed lips and cleared his throat. "I expect you have an opinion and I don't mind if you voice it every once in a while—especially if you think I may be in error."

"Wrong? You, sir? Can't imagine such a thing."

"You'd be surprised. An honest valet is as valuable, if not more, than one who can correctly starch a neckcloth."

"If you say so, sir." The young man chuckled good-naturedly. "Can I be honest with you and speak my mind?"

"I insist upon it." Philip had the feeling he was about to receive his first of both. "Did you have something to say?"

"More of a question, really."

"I shall endeavor to do my best to satisfy your curiosity."

"I've lived in Bloxwich my whole life. I've grown up knowin' the Duke's family plenty while I helped my brother at the Wild Rose." Thomas shifted his weight from foot to foot, with what seemed growing unease. "It's just that I— I've been hearin' talk of Lady Charlotte in the village."

"Gossip, Thomas?" Philip could not help but raise his eyebrows in mild surprise.

"No, sir, I mean to say . . . I'm askin' about her. If it's true or not, about her, that is. They says she's deaf on one side and missin' an eye on the other." His posture stiffened; the accounts clearly disturbed him. "I don't believe it, can't."

"I'm not certain I do either." Philip clapped Thomas on the shoulder. "Think no more about it. Once I find an answer, you can be sure I shall let you know."

He motioned for Thomas to continue on with his duties and then turned toward the house, facing the large Breakfast Parlor window. The movement of the curtains inside falling into place caught his attention. Had someone been there? Watching, perhaps? But they could not have possibly overheard the conversation.

Muriel moved away from the window, pressing her back to the Breakfast Parlor wall. While standing absolutely still, trying to avoid being found out, it dawned on her that she may have misjudged Sir Philip.

While she had caught most of what Sir Philip had said, she did not know to whom he was speaking. What she did catch was the baronet had hired himself a valet.

"Lady Muriel?" Sir Samuel stepped into the Breakfast Parlor. "Are you alone?"

"As you see," she replied at her discovery. Had he entered a moment sooner, he would have caught her spying. How would she have explained that?

"You are up rather early." He looked quite dashing in a frock coat, buckskins, and top boots.

"You are as well," she countered. "Would you care for coffee?"

"Thank you."

She took that as a yes and then heard faint but solid footfalls heading in her direction. Might it be Sir Philip?

Dropping her partially eaten toast on an empty plate, she simply could not occupy a room with him. As rude as she knew it might have been, Muriel quickly told Sir Samuel, "The coffee urn's on the sideboard; please help yourself," before leaving through the servants' door.

Muriel quickly headed toward the terrace, latching the door behind her. She pulled her shawl snug around her shoulders.

"Tom? Tom Sturgis, is that you?" Muriel saw him with a dark brown coat draped over his arm and a pair of boots in hand, heading for the stables. She moved swiftly down the stairs and meant to follow him regardless of his direction.

This is Sir Philip's new valet?

"Yes, m'lady." He stopped, waiting for her. "I mean to say . . . er . . . Lady Muriel."

Tom Sturgis, as far as she knew, helped his elder brother Frank around the stables at The Wild Rose Inn and performed odd jobs. He stood before her well-groomed, well-dressed, and eminently presentable. In his fine light-colored waistcoat and pressed trousers, Muriel nearly did not recognize him.

"Whatever are you doing here?" She'd seen him in Bloxwich on occasion, but never at Faraday Hall.

"It's Thomas now," he amended. "Sir Philip . . . er, that's Sir Philip Somerville, took me on to—" He stopped again and took a great deal of time to compose his reply. "Sir Philip has offered me a position."

"As a valet?" It was an enormous undertaking for the

lad, who was perhaps only a few years younger than Muriel.

"Bit of this and a little of that. If I work hard, take proper care for his wardrobe, and run his errands, he'll learn me how to behave—er, teach me to talk like a right gentleman."

Muriel admired him for wanting to improve himself.

Somehow Charlotte had sensed the goodwill in Sir Philip from the start. Muriel had to admit she'd discovered he was not the completely odious, uncaring man she had once thought.

"I best be movin' along." With a nod of his head, Thomas excused himself and continued on his way. "I bid you good day, Lady Muriel."

Thomas Sturgis had changed before her very eyes. He displayed an enthusiasm and new purpose, and seemed pleased with himself and the new challenge before him. Sir Philip had single-handedly transformed Tom's life, and that made quite an impression on Muriel. Could it be she was losing her dislike for the baronet?

At the top of the stairs, Charlotte straightened the skirts of her morning gown. The household staff was up and about, busy with preparations. Morning calls would soon begin. Flowers from her suitors had been arriving for hours.

Stepping onto the main floor, she admired the lovely daisies, colorful primroses, and the multitude of wildflowers. To view hothouse flowers here in the country would have been a rare thing indeed.

Huxley opened the front door and in walked Susan Wilbanks. "Good day to you, Char-Char."

"Shouldn't you be at home waiting for your young men to call?" Charlotte asked, stepping onto the ground floor.

"Anyone who is in the least desirable will be here, not at Yewhill Grange, I fear. Where is Moo?" Susan untied and removed her bonnet.

"Moo is . . ." Charlotte purposely paused before continuing, and along with Susan said, ". . . reading a book."

"I am so glad you have come, Sukey. I am feeling especially anxious."

"But why? Did you not have a glorious time last night at the Hopkins' ball?"

"Yes, I enjoyed dancing, but there were still so many gentlemen. To have them all pay calls . . ." How could Charlotte explain that she and her sister were trying to *discourage* some of the men. Discourage some they had, but others seemed to take their place.

"There are always loads of visitors. Why should this afternoon be different from any other?" It was not Susan's fault she didn't understand Charlotte's difficulty.

"Ah, Sukey, I thought I heard your voice." Muriel appeared from around the corner of the corridor and set her bookmark in her volume, permanently concluding her morning reading. "Are we ready to face this afternoon's onslaught?"

"Char-Char is having some doubts." Susan took Charlotte's hand in hers, lending some support.

"I am no closer to deciding—" Charlotte stopped and closed her eyes. These last few days had been absolutely maddening. Both Muriel and Susan stared, waiting for her to continue. "As many as we have managed to convince that I may not be exactly who they believe me to be . . . you must admit there are many who still remain."

"What are you talking about, Char-Char?" Susan, who now appeared more confused than ever, turned to Muriel for clarification. "You haven't done something to purposely discourage them, have you?"

"Moo thought it best if we . . . ," Charlotte began. "She had this idea that if I were to—"

"Not here." Muriel glanced around to make certain they weren't seen before suggesting they relocate to her sister's bedchamber to discuss the matter further. "I shall explain our actions to your complete satisfaction momentarily."

Upon entering her bedchamber, Charlotte made for her dressing table to collect a handkerchief to staunch the tears she feared might flow.

"The entire thing's been a *deception*," Charlotte supplied, feeling very guilty.

"Oh no, Char-Char—a test of their affection." Muriel regaled the tales of Charlotte's invented flaws to Susan, which only made her sister feel more dreadful.

After listening, Susan commented to Charlotte, "You weren't trying to hurt them. Do not fret, dear Char-Char. You will manage very well. There are loads of men left."

Muriel moved into the corridor. "Let us find Aunt Penny and we can welcome the gentlemen."

Only minutes later, they found Aunt Penny. The girls, led by Charlotte, descended the stairs, arriving to a near riot.

The nearly two dozen visitors milled about in the Grand Foyer without direction, mumbling to one another in obvious discontent. A number of gentlemen shouted in support of some recent proposed action.

"What shall I do?" Charlotte whispered to her aunt.

"I cannot understand what it is they wish, dear," a confused Aunt Penny relayed to her niece.

"We demand a challenge!" came the shouts of many. "Yes, a challenge! For your favor, Lady Charlotte!"

Muriel could not understand why they should wish to hear of another self-admitted blemish from Charlotte. It was beyond comprehension.

"Gentlemen," Muriel shouted. "Gentlemen!" she repeated louder a second time, raising her hand over her head to gain their attention. "Do calm yourselves, please. Your behavior borders on barbaric."

The room quieted and Muriel spoke freely. "I am sorry to disappoint you. We have nothing planned for this afternoon."

Vehement verbal opposition followed her statement. The gentlemen's voices grew insistent and angry. Muriel knew they would not be satisfied unless this afternoon had a winner.

"What do you suggest then?" she asked the crowd. "Shall we stoop to something as simple as drawing a name out of a hat?"

"My hat!" Lord Paul Bancroft offered.

Major Dunham, looking splendid in his regimentals, cried out, "We can't have that! He's a known cheat!"

"Be warned. I may take offense to that, sir," came the sharp reply from Lord Paul. "We have no time to waste dueling."

"Let it be my hat, my lady!" the dashing Lord Oscar offered.

"No, let it be mine!" Sir Albert Stephenson called out, followed by a few others eager to participate.

The front door opened, and Sir Samuel entered the overflowing foyer and removed his headwear. "What goes on in here?"

"Here, we'll have Sir Samuel's hat," Major Dunham proposed. "He's no involvement in this whatsoever."

"Regarding what?" Sir Samuel replied, baffled at the commotion before him.

"I would appreciate if you would allow us to borrow your chapeau for a game of chance," Charlotte requested in a compelling lilt, one she must have known no male could refuse.

Sir Samuel wore a blissful expression, handing over his curly-brimmed beaver immediately.

"If you would hold it thusly." She turned it in his hand, the brim up and the crown down.

Muriel instructed them all, "Once all of you have placed your calling cards into the hat, we shall begin."

The group parted, allowing Sir Samuel to move from one end of the room to the other. "That's it, gentlemen, cards into the hat," he repeated, moving through the throng.

"What am I to tell them, Moo?" Charlotte whispered to her sister.

"I don't know, Char-Char," Muriel returned quietly. "I had no idea a session of Repelling the Suitors was planned for this afternoon."

"Perhaps I could tell them I am featherbrained or that I am clumsy," Charlotte mused. Could she not think of something better?

"I don't know how that should put them off." Muriel glanced past her sister, keeping watch on the progress of gentlemen beyond.

"No. You're right; it's not enough." Charlotte must think of something much, much worse. "I need something revolting, absolutely horrid. Something that would make them run all the way back to London."

"At least something that would make them reconsider before returning to Faraday Hall," Muriel agreed.

"And I shall," she murmured to herself. "You cannot allow me to face the winner all alone, Moo." Charlotte's stomach churned in agitation.

"You have done it before. Twice, if memory serves." Muriel sounded as if she were going to be quite stubborn.

"I don't think I can manage it again. I feel very uncertain about facing him this time. I wish you would keep watch over me," Charlotte begged her younger sister. "I need to know you're near."

"Observe you? I cannot. You know I cannot." The expression on Muriel's face told how shocking it was that Charlotte should suggest such a thing. "I am forbidden to *eavesdrop* on you."

"I do wish you would. That you might be there to help me . . . just in case—" Charlotte had no idea what she was going to say. What if she couldn't think of anything suitable? Feigning deafness wasn't as great a defect as she had thought. "I give you permission to watch. I insist upon it."

"Very well," Muriel gave in, clearly not pleased. "But I cannot imagine how I should come to your aid if you should need it."

"Thank you so much, dear, dear Moo." Charlotte smiled and exhaled in relief. She would not be alone in this. "I shall meet the winner in the parterre and you shall observe us from the window in my bedchamber."

Finished with his one sweep through the room to collect all the calling cards, Sir Samuel returned to the staircase where the ladies stood.

"Draw the name! Lady Charlotte, draw the name!" came the cries before them.

"Draw *my* name!" one among them shouted.

Charlotte glanced at her aunt, her friend Susan, and finally her sister. She then raised her gloved hand and paused before reaching into the hat. First she mixed the lot with her fingers. The men held their collective breaths. The room fell silent as everyone waited.

The winning calling card emerged, clasped between a thumb and forefinger. Charlotte turned the bold black engraved script toward her and announced, "Lord William Wentworth."

Chapter Thirteen

After a brief retreat abovestairs to fashion her latest ailment, Charlotte proceeded to the parterre. She sat upon the small bench awaiting Lord Wentworth's arrival.

"I must congratulate you on your victory, my lord." Charlotte meant for her tone to be kind.

"I thank you, Lady Charlotte." Lord Wentworth seemed pleased to be in her company. "I am delighted to have the opportunity to learn something about you."

Charlotte glanced away from him and to Muriel, who stood peering down at them from the window, watching every movement, seeing every word spoken through her opera glasses.

"Am I SPEAKING LOUD ENOUGH for you to HEAR ME?" Lord Wentworth forced the uncomfortable words out in varying volumes.

"You need not shout, my lord."

"I beg your pardon." He bowed his head. "I hope I did not offend you."

"No offense was taken." Charlotte glanced back at Muriel, who turned away from the window with obvious laughter. "Please have a seat here next to me." She motioned to the empty space on the bench.

If they both sat facing the house, Charlotte was certain Muriel could see them quite unobstructed.

Lord Wentworth took up Charlotte's hand and held it gently between the two of his. "I must confess that I care not of your false eye or deafness—"

"Deafness?" The allegation took Charlotte by surprise. She'd never said she was deaf.

"You bear each unfortunate affliction with every grace imaginable and have managed to keep them hidden until the brave moment you chose to unveil them. I cannot help but adore you all the more for it—" He gazed at her with much warmth and continued. "If you would assure me of your affection, I would seek out His Grace and beg for permission to offer you marriage this very moment."

"Do not say such things, my lord." Charlotte had not been prepared for this strong sentiment of devotion.

"But it is true," Lord Wentworth exclaimed. "I cannot think of anything but you since the dance we shared last night. I have not been able to eat, drink, or sleep."

"It is fortunate that our acquaintance started only recently, for you should feel very ill if we had been introduced a month ago, or worse, the year before."

"I do apologize. I had not meant to further burden you. I am most anxious to hear of . . ." He glanced at her and immediately fell silent, waiting to hear what she had to say next.

Now Charlotte was the one feeling a bit off. She faced him and in her sweetest voice said, "Well . . . there are times when I am quite . . . clumsy." She glanced up at Muriel, who motioned for her sister to offer him something more than her talent of occasionally treading upon her hem.

Lord Wentworth chuckled. "There is nothing wrong with clumsiness. I'm not proud to admit that, on occasion, I trip over my own feet."

"But the reason for my clumsiness is . . . my limb. My *lower* limb." Charlotte felt her cheeks warm, and no doubt, she blushed ferociously at the utterance of her body part.

He stood. Charlotte followed him to his feet.

Lord Wentworth's jaw dropped open and his eyes bulged. "You cannot mean . . . an *artificial* limb?"

"That is precisely what I mean—" Well, it hadn't been until he made the suggestion. "It's wooden." Charlotte's gaze flew to the window to observe her sister's reaction.

The opera glasses fell from Muriel's face. She slapped her forehead, turned away, and shook her head, eventually moving out of sight.

Oh, dear. Muriel had abandoned her post and Charlotte was quite alone in this now.

"I have seen you on the dance floor. You are flawless." Lord Wentworth reminded her, "I've danced with you myself."

"Yes, it was a cotillion."

"It cannot be true," he muttered. "Ridiculous. I simply cannot believe such a thing."

Charlotte stood and took several steps away from the bench. "It *is* true, I say. See here—" She made a fist and struck the side of her leg, where the unmistakable rap of solid wood sounded. "I've had much practice walking *and* dancing. I only limp a little."

Lord Wentworth stood there unquestionably in shock. He gaped and exhibited some trouble breathing.

"I daresay no one would even know if I'd kept this knowledge to myself." She glanced over her shoulder to check if he had regained his ability to speak. "If any gentleman were serious in forming an attachment to me, I expect they would need to be told."

"I do not . . . I am"—he stared at her skirts, apparently imagining the peg leg under her petticoats—"void of response."

The window of her bedchamber stood empty. Muriel was still not to be seen.

"I do not—" Lord Wentworth cleared his throat and tried again. "If you will excuse me." He performed a swift bow and made a hasty retreat.

Charlotte stood alone in the parterre, next to the bench, and contemplated what she had told him.

What a contemptible tale. Her father would be furious.

Muriel strode from the house toward her sister. "What could you possibly be thinking? Are you mad?"

"You said to think of something that would drive them away. I believe it worked quite well for Lord Wentworth."

"You wished to relay something "very horrid," I be-lieve were your exact words. But honestly, Char-Char, a *wooden* leg?"

"I thought it quite imaginative. Lord Wentworth came up with the idea of a false leg. I had only thought to tell him I was clumsy and tended to stumble about." Charlotte was apparently proud and very pleased with her story. "I should think talk of my wooden leg might send a great deal of the gentlemen away. Isn't that what you wanted?"

Muriel shook her head. "How did you convince Lord Wentworth without resorting to raising your skirt?"

"Oh, that was easy." Charlotte giggled. "I bound one of Freddie's old, broken cricket bats to my leg to remind me which was the afflicted limb."

"Char-Char, how could you?" Even Muriel was taken by surprise.

"This one suited me well because of its shorter length." She raised her hem to display the wooden object attached at her ankle, ending just below her knee. "It also proved quite convincing when I rapped upon it, proving my leg was indeed made of wood."

Charlotte remained seated on the bench alone with her thoughts, mulling over the consequences of her actions a good fifteen minutes following Lord Wentworth's de-parture and nearly five minutes after Muriel had marched away in a huff.

She smoothed the unused lace handkerchief she'd tucked away earlier. Why had she thought there might be need of it? Charlotte had never felt further away from tears than at this moment.

Looking up when hearing the soft crunch of gravel, Charlotte saw the very man she'd wished for appear instantaneously, as if stepping from her dreams. There stood Sir Philip.

With his walking stick in hand, he removed his hat and swept a modest bow in his long, many-caped great-coat.

Charlotte acknowledged his presence with a gracious nod of her head. He moved in her direction, and she rose when he stopped ten feet or so from her.

"Lady Charlotte, do you take the air?" he inquired in a wonderfully sonorous tone.

"I do," she replied. Charlotte did her best to restrain her obvious delight at his company. "You have arrived in time to accompany me for a turn in the rear gardens."

"I am more than happy to oblige." He glanced at his attire. "I must dispense with these travel clothes."

Charlotte stepped to one side, making room for him to deposit his hat, gloves, and greatcoat on the bench where she had been sitting. With a few moments to ensure the pristine condition of his jacket, cuffs, and trousers, he offered her his arm.

She placed her gloved hand upon his sleeve and merely stared at his bare hands. Charlotte wished she were brave enough to touch them.

He glanced around at the meandering pebbled paths, the various garden beds, and beyond to the expanse of countryside that spread out for miles around them. The sight seemed to please him.

"As beautiful as the gardens are, I believe one could grow uneasy after repeating the same route. Passing that small birch grove might become tiresome after the third or fourth time." He looked over at her with a tilt of his head. "Are you not tired of walking this path with every gentleman?"

"That was days ago." So he knew of the garden tours with her suitors. "And I must walk at least once a day for my health. Though I admit walking that particular day was not for my health but to acquaint myself with the gentlemen callers. I only thought it fair for each of them to have the chance to speak to me alone." The topic was an uncomfortable one. Charlotte had no wish to speak to Sir Philip about other gentlemen, and she quickly changed the subject. "I understand you have employed Tom Sturgis."

"Ah, Thomas." Sir Philip smiled. Unless she was mistaken, Charlotte thought she felt an added spring in the baronet's step. "Yes, he's a good lad."

"Yes, but as a valet? I believe he's only cared after horses."

"But he cares for them well, wouldn't you say?"

"I have never heard any complaints—from the equines or their owners. But the point remains, sir," Charlotte was quick to point out, "you are not a horse."

Sir Philip raised her hand to his lips and murmured while looking deep into her eyes, "I am so very glad you have noticed. But horse or no, I could not have competed in your young gentlemen's footrace on the day of my arrival."

By the tone of his voice, he sounded as if he had not approved.

Sir Philip pulled her hand tighter into the crook of his arm. "The damage it may have caused to my boots might have been irreparable."

How easily he could equate the value of her affection with that of his high-topped boots. Then she recalled how her sister went on about Sir Philip and women. Muriel's metaphors of his starched linen strips—carefully crafted cravats indeed! Neither Sir Philip's nor Muriel's analogies pleased Charlotte.

"I am merely a gentleman who has had the misfortune, or in my circumstance, the good fortune, to be stranded in this delightful situation where I can watch the daily sport."

"Sport?" Charlotte stopped, and truth be told, she wasn't pleased with him at the moment. "This is not a game."

"Really? I thought it resembled one at every turn." Sir Philip's hold upon her hand tightened. "The very competitive nature of the participants, the contests, the prizes."

Charlotte had to admit he was correct and that he had consistently refused to allow himself to become involved.

Fine. But why did she feel she needed to use him to measure the other men? In fact, Charlotte cared for the baronet more than she would openly admit. And he . . . compared her with pieces from his wardrobe.

"Dare I make a request of you?" Sir Philip's tone was pleasant.

"You may certainly ask." Charlotte did not think it proper she grant him his every whim, especially when he treated her so dreadfully.

"I fear my time here is coming to an end. I would request you honor us with a song or two this evening after supper. I imagine your aunt and your father, as well as Sir Samuel, would be delighted to hear you play."

"I should like to, if that is what you wish, sir." Even though he had not been particularly kind to her, Charlotte could not bring herself to deny him.

"It is. Above all things." He smiled down at her and stepped forward, continuing their stroll. "I must admit"— a small sigh punctuated his words—"I shall be sorry to leave tomorrow, for I have become quite fond of Faraday Hall and its many pleasant amenities."

Chapter Fourteen

Wooden leg, indeed! What had Charlotte been thinking? Perturbed with her sister, Muriel strode across the terrace to the north side of the house. Perhaps the plan to thin the number of callers was not the wisest, and Muriel's ability to persuade Charlotte should have been employed with a bit more regard.

An old worn wagon sat near the side of house. "Ah, good day to you, Lady Muriel." Farmer Gilbert set an armful of empty wooden boxes on the back of the wagon and drew his cap from his head.

"Good afternoon, Mr. Gilbert."

"Just deliverin' some fresh goods for Sir Philip— some eggs, milk, cheese, and cream."

"I beg your pardon?" Did he say *Sir Philip?*

"We've got what you might call ourselves a gentlemen's agreement, we has."

"I see." Muriel thought this might be a topic she should not trespass upon, being clearly defined as male territory. That had never stopped her before, however, and she continued. "Might I ask what exactly is the nature of this agreement?"

"Bein' you was responsible for our meetin' in the first place"—Farmer Gilbert craned his neck, squinted an eye, and stared over his shoulder at her—"I'll tell you."

Sir Philip had not been amiable to the farmer during their initial encounter. Muriel couldn't wait to hear how the baronet had conducted himself on his subsequent meeting.

"Comin' back from the village, he found me near the same spot the day the two of you came upon me." Farmer Gilbert paused to take a breath. "I was in the briars good—don't know what I would've done if it weren't for him. My plow horse come up lame, you see? Picked up a stone."

If Sir Philip had taken advantage of this man, Muriel would take his fully packed leather trunk and toss it into the pond herself.

"Wanted to know what I did with my lower pasture. Graze my dairy cows, I say to him. He asks me if I'd pasture his horses alongside them. Willin' to pay me, he is. I don't need the blunt—what I need is a horse to hitch to my plow. 'Done,' he says."

"He bought you a horse?" Muriel could not conceive of a thoughtful Sir Philip, much less a magnanimous one.

"Nah, don't know where he got the horse, but it wasn't his. 'On loan,' he says, and wanted me to take good care of him." Farmer Gilbert puffed out his chest, showing pride in his integrity. "I'm an honest man, I am. Don't 'spect no charity, neither."

How had Sir Philip managed that? That was far more than an act of kindness. Muriel glanced around, not wishing to be caught gossiping about Sir Philip.

"I'm to use the horse as a favor to him. That's when we strike a deal—a gentleman's agreement, as Sir Philip says. He knows there's been more than 'spected callers here at Faraday Hall. He wants to help and asks me to contribute on his behalf."

That appeared to be a reasonable solution, and it originated from Sir Philip himself.

"Sir Philip says he leaves it up to my good judgment to decide how much is fair." The farmer waggled his index finger to stress his point. "I ain't gonna take advantage of some city swell. 'N' I'm not about to let him down—he knows that, he does."

"I'm sure he does." Muriel smiled, not quite sure what to think of this newly revealed side of the baronet.

Somehow Charlotte had managed to see this attribute among his exaggerated manners and foppery. Perhaps her sister had been correct about his character. That was too bad. Muriel rather enjoyed thinking Sir Philip wretched.

After much aimless wandering, for she did not know how long she ambled about without Sir Philip, Charlotte approached the double glass doors outside the Music Room. She pressed a dainty handkerchief to her moist nose. Her tear-filled eyes seemed on the verge of overflowing.

Muriel threw the doors open and Susan immediately

ran to her side, lending comfort. "Oh, Char-Char, what is wrong?"

"I do wish Gusta was here. She would know what to do," Charlotte's voice barely choked out.

"You must face facts—Gusta is not here," said Muriel, pulling her sister's hands from her face. "Sukey and I will do what we can. Please tell us. What has happened?"

"Him," Charlotte managed to squeak out.

"I am sorry, to whom do you refer?" Susan could not be faulted for not knowing who might cause Charlotte to weep.

"Sir— Sir— Sir . . ." She could not bear to say his name and uttered simply, "the baronet."

"Tell us which baronet," Susan urged. "Half the eligibles here are baronets. You need to be a bit more specific, my dear."

"There is not a day, an hour, that passes that I do not think of him, wish to see him," Charlotte uttered in hopeful longing, and then paused before managing to allow his name to pass through her lips. "Sir Philip."

Muriel nearly groaned with dread. Charlotte knew her sister did not care for him and, as expected, there would be no sympathy found in that quarter.

"I did not have the pleasure of dancing with him last night as I had hoped." Unable to control her sobs, she wept harder. "He was not meant to be here at all. He does not care for me, you see, Sukey."

"I do not believe there is a single gentleman who would not think you—"

"He was never invited," Charlotte uttered in a soft voice. "Why did he ever come to Faraday Hall? Why did I ever make his acquaintance?" she asked no one in particular.

"Goodness, Charlotte, I have never seen you in such a state," said Susan.

"It is far too clear that he does not have the least bit of interest in me. He has just told me the repair of his curricle is complete and his accounts have been settled. He can think of no reason to remain. As we speak he is making preparations to leave us in the morning." Charlotte could not continue and held her breath to gather her composure. "Do not dare say you are glad of it, Moo."

"I've done no such thing." Muriel must have felt her sister's annoyance.

"You are thinking it, no doubt." Charlotte's anger kept the tears at bay. "I do not think I can bear not seeing him tomorrow, or the next day, or the next . . ." Charlotte didn't know what she was going to do. To tell the truth, she was beginning to feel a bit desperate.

"Your flaw, if I may say, dearest, is that you fall in love too easily," Susan stated.

It was too true. Charlotte gazed at her friend without a smile. "And that is a flaw of such magnitude, I cannot recover."

"But Char-Char, only consider, there are so many other gentlemen who would gladly take *his* place," Susan suggested, trying to point out the good fortune that lay before her.

"Yes, I know. And each of those gentlemen is splendid in his own way. I'm sure it would not matter whom I chose." Charlotte sighed. "But the manner in which I care for Sir Philip is quite different. There is a hidden kindness to him. It is very subtle and one I am unable to ignore."

"I completely agree. I am not likely to forget the likes of him," Muriel added. "Let us go to the Blue Parlor and see who remains."

"I think I ought to tell you both," said Susan, her voice growing timid. "The other gentlemen, they've all gone. Shortly after Lord Wentworth returned, they gathered around him and there was a great commotion before they all left."

Muriel, followed by Charlotte and Susan, headed for the Blue Parlor. There was no one in the corridor, the Grand Foyer stood vacant, and the Blue Parlor was completely deserted.

At one time, the two dozen calling cards from Sir Samuel's hat lay upon the large inlaid rosewood table in the Grand Foyer. Presently, only three remained.

Where were the others? And with the removal of their cards, had those gentlemen withdrawn their interest in Charlotte as well?

"Only three remain." Susan read each: "Mr. Atwater, Lord Stanton, and Sir Hugh Linville."

"That is more than enough. She can marry only one," Muriel reminded them both.

This ruse Charlotte played wasn't supposed to be a game but a means to an end. Not to test them to find the smartest, strongest, bravest man among them, but to find the one man who loved Charlotte for herself.

"But not the one she truly wishes," Susan said with regret.

"I am not sorry in the least for inventing flaws for myself if it has proved that these are the only gentlemen who care for me." Charlotte collected the three cards from the table. "The decision is mine. Allow me to give it some thought." And without another sad sentiment or shed tear, Charlotte climbed the stairs.

"Is she going to be alright?" Susan whispered, sounding concerned for her friend.

"I hope so," Muriel replied with caution. Secretly she hoped her sister would keep her head and not do anything foolish.

Charlotte could clearly hear Sir Samuel and Aunt Penny when she came down the corridor.

"The rate at which the gentlemen callers rush and flee Faraday Hall is alarming," Sir Samuel commented. "I must confess, I've never seen anything like it."

Rounding the corner, Charlotte remained quiet.

Aunt Penny searched the surface of the large round table. "Despite the concerns we discussed, His Grace has instructed me to plan a dinner party for those few who remain." She remained oblivious to her niece's arrival. The search continued around the vase filled with flowers and the small side table next to the Sheraton chairs that lined one wall, and ended at the top of the marble-topped entry table.

"It is understandable," Sir Samuel agreed. "The London Season has been relocated here. I expect one must do their best to replicate the festive atmosphere."

Aunt Penny straightened and appeared confused. "I was certain a few calling cards remained."

Charlotte stepped forward with Huxley following in her wake. "Now that the letters are delivered, we can expect those gentlemen to arrive within the hour. Please have them directed to the hedge maze."

"As you wish, my lady." Huxley acknowledged her instructions with a bow and departed, attending to her request.

Charlotte set the three calling cards upon the circular table and took a moment to move them apart.

"Do I understand correctly that these gentlemen are returning to Faraday Hall?" Aunt Penny asked Charlotte.

"Yes, Aunt Penny." Charlotte stood with an unnaturally stiff bearing. She needed to remain strong. "I have written to each and told them I shall marry the first one who finds me in the center of the maze."

"You did no such thing!" her aunt cried, unable to control her outburst. Sir Samuel caught Aunt Penny's arm, keeping her steady.

"I have," Charlotte insisted. "Since the one gentleman I wish will not have me, it does not matter who else I marry." She glanced down, indicating the three cards on the table with the splayed fingers of her right hand. "I am confident that any one of these more than worthy gentlemen would make a fine husband."

"But Charlotte, this is impossible—" Aunt Penny, who had been robbed of all expression, could not think of what to say to dissuade her. "This cannot be true. You do not mean what you're saying."

"Your sister, Augusta"—Sir Samuel began with complete calm—"had very wise words for me when I found myself in despair after she refused my proposal. At the time, I felt as if I would never find another to return my affection. For I believed myself to be completely . . ."

The emotion that choked his voice came as a surprise. Charlotte had not known he held such esteem for her elder sister.

"I still hold great affection for her, but I do not think I could have made her happy. She assured me that I would someday find someone who would return my regard, and I should not give up hope. I might suggest the same would apply to you." He gazed at Charlotte with heart-wrenching sincerity. "She was quite reassuring and I found myself grateful to her for speaking her mind. It was a difficult subject to broach."

"And how have Gusta's words served you?" Charlotte's voice, although firm, held a small tremor.

"What's that?" he replied, apparently unprepared for her question. He must have been expecting a response from the kind, compassionate Charlotte, not this strong-willed, decisive version.

Charlotte stared at him. She could not see how his circumstance applied to hers. "I believe you find yourself still unattached."

"Well, yes." He glanced at Aunt Penny, who remained silent. "I do, however, expect that someday—"

"Yes, I am sure you shall encounter this woman of mutual affection someday. I tell you now, Sir Samuel, I have met the man I love, and if he cannot declare himself, then it does not matter whom I marry." Charlotte remained adamant and headed for the corridor, toward the rear of the house.

"You cannot mean this." Aunt Penny blanched and clutched onto Sir Samuel's arm even tighter.

Charlotte had not come to this decision lightly. If she did not take this opportunity to choose among the three remaining men, she would never marry. "The letters have already been sent. I shall make my way to Mother's statue in the center of the maze and await my fiancé." Charlotte turned and left.

Sir Samuel stood, supporting Mrs. Parker. "What are we to make of that?" Both of them looked absolutely stunned. "Is there no stopping her? Clearly she is unhappy about her predicament."

Philip heard raised voices, three distinct ones. He moved down the corridor to the staircase, descended the stairs, and joined the two who remained.

"Unhappy? Charlotte has become unreasonable." Mrs. Parker appeared as if she were trying very hard to keep control over her emotions. "I cannot think what to do, Sir Samuel. If you were so good as to help—"

"Anything," he promised. "I am at your service, Mrs. Parker."

Mrs. Parker stepped away from Sir Samuel. "I must inform His Grace at once."

"Is there something amiss?" Philip inquired, revealing his presence in case he had not been noticed. "Might I lend aid?"

There was no disguising her relief at his appearance, or had it been his offer? "I beg your indulgence, Sir Philip. I ask only because we must act quickly." She glanced at Sir Samuel, as if wishing he could explain in her stead. "I am afraid Charlotte has done something—"

"She has promised to marry the first to find her in the center of the maze," Sir Samuel supplied with a succinct expression. "Those gentlemen must not be allowed to enter."

"Yes, that is it exactly," Mrs. Parker agreed.

The news stunned Philip. "Lady Charlotte usually seems most sensible. I do not understand why she would—"

"She is feeling desperate!" Mrs. Parker pulled out a handkerchief to blot her eyes.

Again Sir Samuel intervened. "I believe Lady Charlotte despairs that the man she loves does not return her affection, and therefore it matters not whom she marries."

Philip's brows rose and kept his face impassive so as not to show his surprise. The man she loves? So none of the remaining suitors she wrote were men Charlotte loved.

Could it be . . . ? he wondered.

"I must find the Duke immediately." Mrs. Parker turned

to quit the room. "If you gentlemen will do what you can to prevent those men from entering the maze."

Performing a swift bow, Sir Samuel then headed for the front door.

Philip rose from his somewhat subdued display and replied, "I assure you I shall do my utmost to see these men are prevented from being the first to find Lady Charlotte."

Chapter Fifteen

Charlotte walked from the back of the manor toward the maze. Her steps grew less purposeful and her determination faded when she realized what she had done.

What madness had come over her to promise matrimony to the first man who found her in the center of the maze?

Stopping to lean against the dense privet wall, she pressed her tightly clenched fist to her forehead and closed her eyes.

She had been frustrated and angry at Sir Philip. She'd wished to have him look upon her as her other suitors had . . . not the ones frightened away, but the three who'd remained despite her imaginary flaws.

Then there was her inexcusably childish behavior when she confessed her dissatisfaction to Aunt Penny, right in front of Sir Samuel.

Charlotte tilted her head back and gazed wide into the sky above. As things were, Sir Philip would never know how she felt. He would be long gone by the time she and her new fiancé strolled arm in arm to her father's study to ask permission to marry.

She pushed off the stiff hedge and continued on her way with far less haste, refusing to cry over Sir Philip. Contemplating her remaining suitors, Charlotte decided that any of the three would make a more than acceptable husband. They varied in age and station, but all were from established, wealthy families. All had some pleasing quality to recommend them.

Mr. Atwater was tall with straight brown hair that touched his collar. He had the most delightful twinkle in his eyes when he laughed and enjoyed making her giggle as well.

Lord Stanton enjoyed many of the arts: painting, sculpture, architecture, and music. He delighted in taking walks and admiring the flora as much as she. Charlotte had been introduced to his lordship two years earlier when he came to Faraday Hall for a house party soon after her sister Augusta's first Season. He'd waited for Charlotte to arrive on the social scene, and then stood in her long line of suitors for a chance to pay his addresses.

The green-eyed, fair-haired Sir Hugh Linville, youngest of the three, was the most handsome and had a very charming smile. She adored his constant optimistic outlook. His dancing skills were exceptional. She recalled that he'd been the first to arrive with a filled pail of gooseberries.

Finally reaching the center of the maze, Charlotte settled onto the stone bench. She busied herself by arranging her skirts to make a favorable impression. When regret slowly seeped into her heart and soul, she then allowed her eyes to close. No matter how good, kind, or agreeable those men were, they were simply not meant for her.

Charlotte pressed her hand to her mouth and choked back a sob, realizing she should not have written those letters.

In times when she felt in particular need of her mother, Charlotte would come to this place, wishing the late duchess were still with her. A mother she barely remembered. But the words came to her as if her maternal parent had said them herself.

Make it right.

Yes, Charlotte vowed. Perhaps she would break one more heart before the day was through. She would explain to *him*, when he arrived . . . whoever *he* should be, that she had made a mistake. She would offer a most sincere apology to him, hope he would understand, and confess that she had no intention of marrying.

Settled in her favorite chair in the Librarium, Muriel expected Susan's arrival at any moment. A knock sounded at the open door, echoing off the book-lined walls of the room before someone entered. Not Susan, but to Muriel's great surprise, there stood Sir Philip.

"I beg your pardon, Lady Muriel." He stepped forward, dressed for travel in a brown frock coat, buckskins, shiny top boots, and if she was not mistaken, a bit of humility. "I must speak to you on a matter of some urgency. This is in regard to your sister."

Muriel could not believe he was here, in her private sanctuary.

"It seems that in her distress, Lady Charlotte had penned some letters to her remaining suitors, agreeing to marry the first to find her in the center of the maze."

"That is not true." Muriel launched to her feet. It could not be. She moved around the table and made to dash past the baronet, out the door, to find Charlotte and hear it for herself.

"Not so fast." Sir Philip put up his arm, blocking the doorway and preventing her exit.

"Allow me to pass, sir," Muriel glared. "If what you say is true—"

"Do not fear. Mrs. Parker is at present notifying your father, and Sir Samuel keeps watch for the gentlemen's arrival."

"And you're here? Was it your task to inform me?" Muriel backed away from him. His presence, not to mention his proximity, upset her.

"No, I wish to successfully traverse the maze." It did not appear Sir Philip was joking.

"You?" This could not be happening. Muriel knew he'd heard the rumors regarding Charlotte. How could he possibly overlook the talk of the men who had seen her imperfections for themselves? "But why?"

"Because I find myself in love with her—and if it matters not to her whom she weds, why should she not marry me?"

At one time Muriel had to admit she did not care for him. However, he'd befriended Mr. Evans, employed

Thomas Sturgis, and had come to Farmer Gilbert's aid—perhaps even saving his farm. She'd begun to think of the baronet differently.

"Unless I am much mistaken, Lady Charlotte is under the impression I care little or nothing for her, because I have not behaved in a manner that accurately expressed my affection." He came around the table displaying much confidence.

His imposing bearing even impressed Muriel. Not what she had expected at all.

"I was, at first, as you might imagine, drawn to her, just as the others had been, by her beauty."

Why did he feel the need to be honest, especially to her? It made his actions respectable, and Muriel had no wish to have her already altered opinion of him elevated.

"I was an unexpected participant in a conversation with Mrs. Parker and Sir Samuel regarding your sister a short while ago." Sir Philip looked down his nose at Muriel while speaking. "I deduced from their abstract reference that I, without their knowledge, might have been the implied subject. I believe I am the gentleman who had not declared his affection for Lady Charlotte and caused her to behave . . . out of character."

Muriel glared back. Was he taking responsibility for Charlotte's rash action?

"I imagine if it were up to you, I would have never discovered it."

"Me?" Muriel had done what she could to keep them apart, though she was not yet ready to admit it.

"I have come to realize that you are her true protector, not her father, His Grace, nor her aunt, Mrs. Parker."

"I am only a girl, a child of fifteen."

He chuckled. "You may be only fifteen, but you are not a child. You are an imp, a most precocious imp, if I am not mistaken. I do not underestimate your influence upon your sister, nor your ability to outmaneuver any person you choose."

Muriel shrugged. "You give me far too much credit, sir."

"I do not believe I do," Sir Philip stated with certainty. "Even with my practiced sensibilities and mastery of decorum, I can restrain myself no longer. *You*, my girl"—he glared at her—"are a meddling bluestocking!"

"Meddling?" Muriel gasped. Indeed, she had been. "Well, *you*, sir, are a pompous prig!"

"I beg your pardon!" he said, enunciating every word and finishing with a slight widening of his eyes. "You mistake my concerted effort to accomplish the deeds I consider important. Whereas, I'm sure, you come by your talent naturally."

And he was correct. Muriel had to admit that she did not hold the same opinion of him as she had the day before or that very afternoon, for that matter. Still, he could be unpleasant. "You behave as if you are far superior to any of Charlotte's men."

"I am not better than any other gentleman," Sir Philip replied with all the arrogance Muriel had expected. "I simply *dress* better."

Her eyelids slid closed and she could not prevent herself from thinking him dreadful.

"We do not have time for further discussion—your sister awaits her future husband and the gentlemen grow closer to Faraday Hall. I cannot allow them to find her—*I* adore her." He laid his hand upon his heart and spoke with sincerity. "Yes, she is beautiful, but that is not what compels me to seek her. It is her irresistible inner beauty."

Muriel had done what she could to prevent the baronet from discovering Charlotte's good qualities for himself. As it turned out, it seemed that nothing would discourage him.

"She had more than enough suitors from which to choose," he continued. "Any one of them would have been a suitable, no, an adequate match. Yet she does not choose among them. She does not wish to marry merely a handsome, nor a wealthy, titled peer. Lady Charlotte wishes for much, much more. Someone who would love her for herself."

No one had told Sir Philip of their strategy. How could he have discovered it on his own?

"So you came up with a plan to test them. Rumors of a glass eye, deafness, and a wooden leg then circulated through the ranks. Your doing, I suspect." Sir Philip nodded in her direction, acknowledging her involvement.

Muriel hated to admit he was correct, but she had not thought up all Charlotte's flaws. How could he have known?

"The truth?" he mused, taking in a breath and narrowing his eyes. "Dear, sweet Charlotte is too kindhearted and considerate of their feelings. She cannot bear to turn any of them away. I believe she cannot be truly happy with anyone who remains. I expect you already know that as well."

"You are impertinent, sir." Muriel could not take all the credit or blame. "How do you know the rumors are not true?"

"Oh, come now." He chuckled. "I am not like the young pups who have lost their ability to think, as have the bulk of Lady Charlotte's suitors. Despite her obvious beauty, she has the rare ability to see the goodness in anyone and is in possession of a compassionate soul. Those are qualities, I must confess, I find compelling." Sir Philip rubbed his eyes and his gaze dropped to Muriel.

She strongly suspected Sir Philip's affection for Charlotte. Muriel simply had not wished to acknowledge it existed. She also knew of Charlotte's certainty that he was the man she truly loved.

"And I think she has the most wonderful sister—devoted, protective, if not a bit sinister. You were trying to save her from me, weren't you? No matter who among the other suitors would be discouraged, or what small lies needed fabricating."

"You are an out-and-out bounder. What you say is pure conjecture."

There was no trace of laughter from Sir Philip now. "You judged me by my exterior. It is the very same egregious error those men made who wished Charlotte for their own."

"They didn't love her," said Muriel. "When they discovered she was not the perfection they believed, they left." Muriel was right, about most of them, anyway. Yet here was Sir Philip trying to convince her of his affection for Charlotte. "I do not understand why you bother yourself by speaking to me. Shouldn't you beg for an audience with my father?"

"Ah." Sir Philip raised his index finger, pausing for a moment. "I may need his approval for marriage, but I believe I need yours to be successful in my pursuit." He turned to gaze at Muriel. "If I am the first to arrive, then, by her own admission, it is me whom she must wed."

"In any case, I am not needed." Muriel conceded that he was indeed very clever to puzzle their plan out.

"Could you, would you, come to my aid?" he pleaded.

"You want me to help you cheat?" She narrowed her eyes. He was asking the impossible. "Why should I do such a thing?"

"Without your guidance, I would certainly be lost in the maze. Unless I am fortunate enough to stumble upon the center—and this is far too important to leave to chance."

This man stood tall, and seemingly strong, but Muriel knew if she refused to help him he would crumple before her eyes. How fragile he seemed to her all of a sudden.

"I would cherish her always," he vowed in all sincerity. "Because I am not the man you thought I was, because I am the man who dearly loves your sister. Please consider that my future, and your sister Charlotte's future, rests in your hands." Sir Philip's gaze did not waver from Muriel.

The momentous weight of her sister's future happiness sat heavily upon her. Muriel had not been prepared to make this decision.

What was she to do? She did not have the luxury of time for contemplation. She thought of Charlotte in the center of the maze waiting for one of her suitors to arrive. Someone she promised to marry, someone she did not completely love. And here stood Sir Philip. Had he successfully convinced Muriel of his love for Charlotte?

Muriel collected paper and pencil and returned to the table. She quickly sketched the route to the center of the maze and handed it to him.

"I thank you," he murmured, accepting what amounted to him as a treasure map. "One last thing. It would also be of great value if you were to help divert the other three."

"You must think me mad," Muriel whispered to him, "for I certainly believe I am for coming to your aid."

"No, I think you love your sister, as do I." Sir Philip gave her a reassuring smile and then left.

Chapter Sixteen

Muriel accompanied Sir Philip down the stairs to the rear terrace, where they parted. With the map she had drawn for him in hand, he continued toward the maze.

With the directions, she guaranteed he would be the first to find Charlotte and, no doubt, convince her they should wed. Her fate was now out of Muriel's hands. Charlotte would have her chance, if Sir Philip was the man she wished for her husband.

She headed for the front drive, where visitors, if they were to arrive, would first appear.

"Moo!" Susan called out to her from the shady north side of the house.

Muriel dashed forward to meet her friend. "Has there been any sign of the—"

Sir Samuel came pelting around the front corner of the house and slid to an ungainly stop before them. "Three riders on horseback, about three, perhaps four minutes apart, approach as we speak."

Sir Philip had only just entered the maze. Muriel realized the gentlemen would need to be delayed. The three moved to a position from which they could view the riders.

"It's Sir Hugh Linville," Sir Samuel announced when the first came into sight.

The trio moved back, so as not to be seen.

"He always was keen on arriving early," Muriel mumbled.

"Shall we tell them there's been a mistake?" Sir Samuel offered.

That might well have been a solution, but Muriel did not think it quite right.

"No, we can't do that. Think of the scandal!" Susan stared from Sir Samuel to Muriel with unease.

Yes, that was the problem—the potential for the family's disgrace.

"I do not think we should prevent them from entering the maze. But let us be clear on this"—Muriel met both Susan's and Sir Samuel's gazes, making sure all three of them were in perfect agreement—"we do not want any of these gentlemen to succeed."

"But if you allow them to enter the maze, will they not find the center eventually?" Sir Samuel appeared puzzled.

"No, they will not," Susan assured him. "There is a trick to finding the center, you see? Each of the entrances has their own way to—"

"We don't have time for explanations, Sukey." Muriel turned to Sir Samuel. "Greet Sir Hugh, if you will, and see him to the Elephant entrance of the maze. It's past the Giraffe, on the north side. You must convince him it is the way to the center."

"It's not, correct?" Sir Samuel's gaze wandered to Susan for an answer.

"Do not waste time," Muriel urged him. "Go!"

Sir Samuel acknowledged his instructions with a nod and left. The scatter of gravel sounded with his every step. He soon disappeared around the corner of the manor.

A few moments later, he rounded the corner once again, sliding to a stop before them to say, "Mr. Atwater has just turned onto the drive." Away again he dashed, returning to welcome Sir Hugh.

"Sukey, you must direct Mr. Atwater to the Camel entrance and bid him good luck."

"Very well." Susan shared a very small devious smile with her friend. Growing up with the sisters, Susan knew exactly how the maze worked and would keep the secret to herself.

"I will see Lord Stanton to the Giraffe entrance." Muriel clasped Susan's hands and together they walked toward the drive. "Do not fear, Sukey; everything will work out as it should."

"I hope so," Susan replied with a tone filled with hope. She glanced at Muriel before leaving her side to greet Mr. Atwater.

Muriel stood alone, watching Lord Stanton's high-spirited bay turn from the main road onto the drive. While waiting for his arrival, fleeting thoughts of Sir

Philip and the directions she'd given him through the Lion opening occupied Muriel.

The easiest entrance, she thought. He would not need to crawl through the hidden underground tunnel, find the small passage only fit for children, or locate the impossible-to-find door that on occasion was overgrown and impassible.

In short, if the baronet had followed her instructions, he should be arriving at the maze's center just about now.

After passing the entrance, Philip made his way down the manicured path, making the indicated turns until he came to the supposed "hidden ladder." He pressed his hand into the foliage wall, setting his boot on the lowest rung. Then he went up.

Once he arrived on the other side, he consulted his map again. The center of the maze, and Lady Charlotte, stood on the other side of his hedge wall. He imagined her lovely smile and her wide, blue eyes staring at him.

He took a few moments to compose himself. In preparation to face her he adjusted his cuffs and plucked at his cravat. Then he knocked off the stray bits of debris from his buckskins and sleeves. Philip stepped out from around the corner.

"Sir Philip!" Charlotte cried out in surprise and drew back at his sudden appearance. "I thought you were . . . someone else."

"One of your many gentlemen suitors, perhaps?"

She need not make the confession regarding the letters she'd written, and answered him with a shy nod.

"I am sorry to disappoint you; it is only I." Philip performed a sedate bow, with a sweep of his right arm as the only flourish.

Although his arrival had been unexpected, Charlotte did not behave as if she were disappointed to see him. If only she realized he was here because she had promised to wed the first gentleman who found her and Philip had hoped to claim that prize.

Not wishing to further frighten her, he politely inquired, "Would you mind if I remained until their arrival?"

"I welcome your company, sir. It is very thoughtful." Releasing the fistfuls of material she clutched, Charlotte smoothed her skirts. "I was under the impression you were making preparations to leave us."

"I fear I may be delayed." Had she any knowledge he'd postponed his departure on her account?

"Really?" Her reply implied interest, not regret, over his setback.

"Over the past few days I have been occupied with the repair of my curricle and arranging appropriate reimbursement to those who have been kind enough to come to my aid. Only this afternoon have I realized an unforeseen event that might detain me for far longer than . . ." Philip drew in a breath, realizing the importance of the next fifteen minutes. His discussion with Charlotte could alter his future, depending on the outcome.

"I wish you every success in finding an adequate resolution, then. It would be a shame to delay you any longer then need be."

There would be no shame in speaking honestly. He had to declare himself, his affection to her. If by chance Charlotte did not share his feelings . . . It would not matter. If he did not speak his mind, his heart, he had no doubt it would be a lifelong regret.

In a mere half dozen strides he crossed with ease to the center and lifted his quizzing glass to examine the statue.

"I must say this statue has the most exquisite workmanship." He studied the marble with great care. "She seems almost lifelike—as if she might step down from her plinth at any moment."

Charlotte wondered why he had never gazed at her that closely or examined her with similar interest. It was as if he purposely paid her no notice when they were together. She could not imagine why he should do such a thing.

"Is she a relation?" he inquired. "Your—"

"Mother," Charlotte finished, easing onto the stone bench, wishing he would sit beside her. "Her name was Sarah."

"I imagine she was every bit as lovely as you." Sir Philip pivoted from the statue to Charlotte. "I wonder if she had experienced . . ."

Charlotte gazed up at him. "What is it, Sir Philip?"

"I must confess, while I was in the village I heard rather unflattering and unpleasant accounts regarding your—" Sir Philip stopped short of mentioning the details that were all too familiar to Charlotte. "I'm certain the tales were completely unsubstantiated."

"Regarding me?" It had not taken long for word to spread among the gentlemen. Muriel had been correct.

"Do you mind if I have a look for myself and form my own opinion on the matter?" He waved his quizzing glass in her direction.

"What is it you wish to examine?" She blinked at him. Sir Philip proved not to be immune to the gossip, in any case. Here he was now, asking to verify what he'd heard for himself, and Charlotte wondered if he would think any less of her to discover it true.

"I hope I am not being indelicate." He concealed his polite cough with the back of his hand and moved closer to the bench. "I hear tell you have a glass eye."

"Oh, that." Charlotte swallowed and looked away. She had the distinct feeling she should not meet his gaze.

Sir Philip put his quizzing glass to his eye and leaned near to better inspect hers, coming much closer to Charlotte than she felt comfortable. Her face warmed and her heart raced. She had some difficulty drawing breath.

He wore no gloves, which gave Charlotte a chance to study his long, slender fingers clasping the handle. All that lay between them was the thin lens of his accessory. She stared straight ahead, allowing him to examine her eyes, the right one first, and then the left. Charlotte forced herself to look away from him.

Moving from her right eye to her left, he brushed a wayward strand of hair with his fingertips. It was merely a courtesy gesture, one to move the bothersome curl from her face. In doing so, he accidentally touched her cheek, which caused her to shiver at his contact.

"They are a most delightful blue, I must say." His voice was soft, and she could hear a hint of a smile within. "And if I were to hazard a guess, they are an exact color match. They could not be more perfect!" He straightened, moving away from her. "I am astonished at the miracles of glass that can be achieved nowadays. Do you think having a glass eye bothers some of your suitors? I can't imagine that it would matter. You've still got one good one."

"I cannot say, sir," she replied, again not meeting his gaze directly.

"Are you certain your eye is false? It appears quite normal."

She had no choice but to convince him otherwise. Charlotte focused on twitching her eye, moving it incrementally further to the right.

"Goodness . . . ," he remarked with concern, more curious than frightened. "Your eye is . . . ah . . . gone a bit off." He gestured to his left with his quizzing glass.

"Oh!" Charlotte blinked and thumped the side of her head. "I beg your pardon; it does that on occasion."

"Amazing. Quite astonishing." He dropped to the ground on one knee before her, with no apparent regard to his apparel.

"Sir!" she cried out. "Take care, you shall certainly ruin your—AH!" Charlotte recoiled but could not move far. Sir Philip had a firm hold of her right ankle. "What do you think you are doing?"

"I was merely authenticating the rumor of your wooden leg." He glanced at her and flashed a smile. "Appears to be a hum, if you ask me."

"You could have inquired." She pushed against his shoulder, wishing he would remove his hand from her lower extremity. "At least requested permission before taking liberties."

"Posing questions before making a questionable maneuver would eliminate the delightful surprise element." Sir Philip finally released his hold of her ankle and then moved to lean over her left shoulder.

"I must tell you that my conscience compels me to speak my mind," he whispered into her left ear. "I must confess how ardently I admire you."

"You *care* for me?" Charlotte could hardly believe what he was saying. It was everything she wished to hear.

"How extraordinary!" Sir Philip proclaimed. "Another rumor proved erroneous. I'd heard you were deaf in your left ear." He lifted his quizzing glass to regard her appendage. "Couldn't hear a thing."

"Oh, do stop that." She slapped his hand, knocking the accessory—which should have flown from him if not for the ribbon tethering it to his neck.

He snatched her wrist and held it fast. Charlotte gasped at the contact and stared at him, absolutely shocked at his audacity at again touching her uninvited.

"I will admit you are a beauty, but it is not that which

truly interests me. It matters not how many faults you disclose, for the kindhearted, caring soul you possess is a treasure true." He lowered himself onto the bench next to her and continued, "I have heard how you had come to the aid of the citizens of Bloxwich and Farmer Gilbert's family in particular."

"Oh, that." Someone had had to intervene, for the family was in dire straits. Circumstances dictated that she should act, for she had been present at that precise time.

"You are an amazing woman—and I find if I do not control myself, I should take advantage of this opportunity that we are alone and kiss you," he murmured softly.

"I hardly think that gentlemanly conduct at all!" Charlotte said, shocked that he would even suggest it. What type of a man was he? What kind of a lady did he think she was to allow such behavior?

"Do you not feel anything for me? Perhaps you think of me as one of your many suitors and no more. Someone to be tested, sent on quests, and do your every bidding in an effort to fetch your favorite savory, find a missing gewgaw, or perhaps cruelly tease for your sheer amusement."

"That is not true. I find you . . ." Charlotte finally found the strength to meet his stare. How wonderful it felt to finally tell him the truth. "You are more than acceptable, sir. It is only . . . what if I were to allow every gentleman who wanted to kiss me to do so?" She leaned back to regard him at a more respectable distance but could not move far. "I believe that would be most inappropriate, sir. Such activity should be reserved—only allowed between a husband and wife."

"And why do you think I am here, my girl?" A slow smile graced his lips. "I had heard you vowed to wed the first gentleman to find you in the center of this maze. Have I not done just that?"

"But how could you have known?" Charlotte could not imagine how he had discovered it, but beyond that, she realized that he wanted to marry her.

"There is not much which concerns you that remains private." Sir Philip held her hand, drawing it close.

"You need not hold me to my promise, for I care more for you than any other gentlemen, even if I had to choose from all the men in England."

"Actually, I believe you did." Sir Philip brought her hand to his face and pressed it to his cheek. "Will you do me the honor, then, of becoming my wife?"

Yes, she thought, but could not manage to speak her mind. Charlotte knew her opinion of Sir Philip was not the only one that mattered.

"I do not know how I could accept when, I am sorry to say, my sister Muriel does not care for you."

"Ah, yes, the irascible Lady Muriel. My task has been arduous. Not only did I need to win your heart, I needed to seek her approval first."

"She knows you are here?" Charlotte found it impossible to believe Muriel would ever consent to Sir Philip turning his affection to Charlotte.

"You see, I secured directions from Lady Muriel herself." He released her hand to pull a folded piece of paper from the pocket of his waistcoat. Unfolding it revealed a map drawn in pencil. "I imagine that would have proved more difficult than speaking to His Grace for permission to pay my addresses."

Charlotte giggled into her hand. "Muriel can be difficult." But she was so happy! The map was by her sister's hand, which meant Muriel must have approved of the baronet.

"Now that we have your sister's blessing in regards to our future, I would very much like to kiss you."

"Then, sir, I should have to accept, for I, too, wish you to kiss me." Charlotte smiled and leaned toward him for her reward.

"Ah!" he interrupted, stopping her progression.

"What's wrong?" She froze.

"Shall we wait until after we speak to His Grace or do we dare cross the line of propriety and kiss before we are even officially engaged?"

Sir Philip enveloped her hand with his own. His hand felt warm, his touch tender, and he remained silent as if debating the matter.

"I think not," he murmured after some thought. Sir Philip lowered their clasped hands, stared into her face, and smiled. "I care too much for you to endanger your reputation. It will already come under scrutiny, as we are presently unchaperoned."

He pressed a kiss to the back of her hand. Charlotte felt her knees weaken and realized she'd been struck momentarily speechless.

"Let us seek out your father, shall we?" Sir Philip helped her stand, tucked Charlotte's hand into the crook of his arm, and led the way out of the maze. "You are aware once we emerge that we take the risk of having litigious rumors being spread about us?"

"Rumors?" Charlotte giggled. "You better than anyone should know one cannot always believe everything one hears."